Never Cross A Boss 4

Trust Issues Book 4

Tamicka Higgins

© 2017

Disclaimer

This book contains sexually explicit
content that is intended for ADULTS ONLY
(+18).

Chapter 1

Marcus and Kayla had agreed to meet up at the White Castles at the intersection of Keystone Avenue and 38th Street. Marcus knew the neighborhood well, almost too well. He was somewhat glad that his mother was taking him over to this area to meet with Kayla in the morning rather than late afternoon or night. The last thing he wanted to happen right now was for people to see him, especially since he was meeting with Kayla.

The feeling of guilt grew so much inside of Marcus that it almost began to make him sick. Not only could he believe how much Kayla's life was in danger when his apartment got shot up, but now she was practically hiding from the very nigga that was after Marcus. Furthermore, Marcus was practically torn on what seemed like the long ride across the east side on 38th Street. While his eyes could not help but to scan the faces of niggas walking up and down the street, or coming out of strip malls that they drove by, his mind was wondering what exactly would be Kayla's reaction to him. Since dropping him off at his mother's house just last night, which seemed so long ago at this point, her life had changed so much. Her mother, brother, and sister had been held hostage by a couple of niggas with guns. Marcus knew that he did not know what something like that felt like, so he would need to be extra cautious when it came to meeting with Kayla inside of the White Castles restaurant.

Lorna must have been reading her son's mind at that very moment. After what had been several long minutes of them driving down East 38th Street, Lorna broke the silence.

"What's on your mind, Marcus?" she asked. "You thinking about what you're going to say when you see Kayla?"

Marcus looked at his mother. He hated how there were moments he felt like she could really read his mind. And this was turning out to be one of those moments.

"How you know that?" Marcus asked, turning and looking back at the street as they crossed Sherman Avenue, the last main street before they would come to Keystone a couple of miles down the street.

"Cause," Lorna said. "I know that's what I would be thinking."

"I just feel helpless," Marcus said.

Lorna instantly turned down the DMX album that she had playing in the background. She always wanted to be the kind of mother that actually listened to her child. This way, she would know what her child was thinking so she could know when she needed to talk to him – pick her battles wisely, so to speak. "Why you say that, Marcus?" Lorna asked. "What's on your mind, son?"

"Just I feel helpless, like I said," Marcus answered. "I got my arm in a sling and all wrapped up and stuff while some nigga – I mean dude – is out there trying to get me and my girl."

"Well," Lorna said, knowing that this was another one of those perfect times to teach him a valuable lesson. "I hate to be the one to tell you this, but I always told you this, so I might as well anyway right now. Those are the kinds of risks that you take when you choose to live that kind of life, unfortunately. Generally, for most dudes, just like some of the ones that I went to high school with, living that kind of life and making your money that way tends to be just a dead-end road. The sooner a lot of these black men out here understand that, as well as these women who like getting with them and going along with it just because he buys you nice things, the better off we all will probably be. That's just how I feel, sorry. But, please give some thought to what I said. Maybe this could be a new chance – a new start over. I talked to your uncle and he's going to see what he can do about this. Hopefully, with the people he knows and how long he's been out there doing it, basically since we both were your age and stuff, he can talk to this Hakim or whatever his name is. If not, time and distance are the only options you have. I feel for Kayla, though. I really do, Marcus."

That last sentence kind of hit a sore spot with Marcus. His guilt virtually made every word sound more pronounced. Marcus could not imagine losing his girl Kayla to something that was not even her fault. He looked back at the situation and really wished, deep down, that he had never gone against his Uncle Roy – that he had kept everything he did within the family, rather than going outside of it, like Roy had always taught him. When he drove to and from Texas, and smashed Hakim's chick Tweety in his own house, he never for one second thought that his life would wind up like this. Yesterday, he had almost been killed, as well as Kayla. Now he and Kayla were meeting at a White Castles near where she was staying, before he headed up to stay with his cousin Larry in Fort Wayne. Life is so fragile, Marcus thought, remember how his great-grandfather used to tell him that before he passed when Marcus was a teenager. At the time, he did not know what it meant. However, as he grew into a man, he quickly learned and picked up on exactly what his great-grandfather meant. And it was scary at this point, especially as he looked down at his arm.

"Yeah," Marcus said, now seeing the White Castles sign some blocks up ahead. "This is pretty bad. I gotta talk to Kayla in person."

"Well," Lorna said. "Just think, as you're talking, how you go about talking to her. I would imagine that, right now, she is probably even more scared than you are. You at least are heading out of town – getting out of dodge for whatever that man has planned. She does not, however. She is staying wherever you said, over here at Thirty-Eighth and Keystone, with her family. I can only imagine how scared they all must be, going through something as traumatic and messed up as someone coming into your house and holding you and your family hostage. To only make matters worse, in a way, they really can't go back home because…because…because they just don't know when it will be safe. And you did somewhat cause this. I'm your mother, so I'm not going to let you think that you're just the victim. You're not and I want you to understand that."

"I do," Marcus said. "I do."

Within what seemed like seconds, Lorna was turning the car into the parking lot of the White Castles at 38th and Keystone Avenue. As usual, dudes dressed in black hoodies stood around out on the sidewalk and on the outer edges of the parking lot. After Marcus scanned the faces of each and every dude standing around the doors of the restaurant, he then looked around for Kayla.

"Where is she?" Marcus asked, without even realizing that he was talking out loud.

Lorna pulled into a parking spot. "Maybe she's waiting inside," she said. "You wanna go on in there and see if you see her or wait for her? You can sit with her for half an hour or so, if you want, while I run right down to this store we passed on the way here. If you guys need more time, just call me and tell me or text me or whatever. Just don't be too long, though. You know how this part of town can get once everybody wakes up. It's still kind of early, so we should be okay. Just watch yourself."

"Aight," Marcus said, as he climbed out of the car and headed into the restaurant.

As soon as Marcus stepped into the restaurant, the smell of breakfast combined with the place just having changed over to lunch immediately hit him. His eyes scanned the booths and chairs of the restaurant, looking beyond the short lines fanning away from the glassed-in cash register. The workers zipped around in the back, in the kitchen area, dressed in their blue uniforms and black visors. For a brief second, Marcus thought about a time where he had turned down a job offer to work at a different White Castles location. Now that he thought about it, the offer came from a buddy he went to school with right around the same time he started to get serious out in the streets. He was working under the wings of his Uncle Roy, so to speak. In hindsight, with a shoulder that had been shot almost 24 hours ago, Marcus sort of wished that he had chosen the fast food job. Sure, he could have been shot in that, such as in a robbery or something. However, he probably would not have to worry about somebody being after him because of it.

Marcus snapped out of his tiny trance when he noticed that Kayla was walking into the restaurant on the other side. Not even paying much attention to the other people sitting in the restaurant, or the people in the lines, Marcus made his way across the restaurant. Without even speaking, he and Kayla embraced. They hugged one another, standing in the doorway of the restaurant door. Marcus never thought that he would miss his woman so much as he did right at that very moment. When they broke away from their hug, they kissed one another briefly.

"Here," Marcus said. "We can go sit over there."

Marcus guided Kayla over to a booth, off to the side of the restaurant. Cars zipped by the window as they pulled into the drive through lane. Kayla slid into the booth, now across from Marcus. Immediately, he noticed how unusually quiet she was. Kayla was almost what many would describe as being reserved. Marcus could feel how cold she was, hearing her silence.

"You alright?" Marcus asked.

Kayla nodded then shrugged her shoulders. "As aight am I'mma be, I guess," she said.

Marcus nodded, hearing the tension in her voice. It was clear to him that everything that happened yesterday, then last night, had essentially broken his woman's spirit. And he hated to think of that because he knew that it all came back to him and his actions. He pushed passed the guilt that he was feeling, wanting to make the most of the little time he would have in the restaurant with her. He looked around outside for a moment, then focused his attention back to Kayla, across the table from him.

"I'm sorry, Kayla," Marcus said to her. He knew why he was saying sorry, but did not know if Kayla would know why he was saying. This is why he felt the need to explain. "All of this is my fault and I feel horrible about it. How is your mother? How is Latrell and Linell?"

Kayla shrugged and said okay. "I don't know," Kayla said. "When I left the house to walk the couple of blocks up here, my mama was up. She ain't say much, though. And I can tell that the side of her head still hurtin' her from where that nigga hit her in the head with his gun."

Marcus sucked air in through his teeth. He could practically feel the pain his own self when he thought about how it must feel to be pistol whipped in the side of the head.

"That's fucked up, Kayla," Marcus said. "I swear to God that is some fucked up shit."

"Yeah," Kayla said, kind of avoiding eye contact. "We stayin' at my mama's friend's house down the street. I don't know this neighborhood like that. I've only passed through over here when I was either coming from your place or going to my cousin's house up off of Fifty-Sixth Street or something. I ain't really sleep well. I guess cause I keep feelin' like them two niggas are gon' come knockin' at the door."

"I swear to you, Kayla," Marcus said. "I'mma do everything I can to make sure that don't nothin' happen to you. My mama said that my uncle try'na get in touch with Hakim and shit to see if he can help with this or not."

"Yeah," Kayla said. "But you leavin' me today, leavin' the city, to go hide up in Fort Wayne."

"Don't say it like that," Marcus snapped back. "Don't act like I'm a nigga runnin' out of town to hide or nothin'."

"Then what are you doing, Marcus?" Kayla asked, sounding very matter of fact. "Huh? What are you doing? It sure look like you goin' out of town to hide. And I get it…I really do. But what about me? Whoever the fuck this nigga is that say you fucked him over done sent two niggas to my house and held my family at gunpoint and shit. That shit was so scary that I could not even begin to describe how it felt to walk through the door and see that shit when I got home last night from dropping you off over at your mama house. Now, they after me cause I lied to them and told them that you was still in the hospital when I knew you wasn't. You shoulda seen how they was lookin' at me…some of the shit that they said about my body before they left to head down to the hospital."

Immediately, Marcus' mind took him back to the little chat he had with Hakim last night. He cringed just thinking about some of the things that Hakim had said to him about Kayla's body. And he hated that he could not take her with him to protect him. Nonetheless, he was not going to make her feel any better by telling her something like that.

"Kayla, listen to me," Marcus said. He slid his hands onto the table and reached out and held hers, softly. "I know I'mma be out of town and be low for a minute," he said. "But I swear to God, as soon as I get cool and shit, I'mma get my boys on this shit and everything. I ain't tell my mama, but I was kinda thinkin' bout how I'mma get Hakim."

"Marcus," Kayla said. "You can't be serious. How you gon' get Hakim? You gon' be up in Fort Wayne, and you only got one arm. I was at the hospital and stuff. I remember when they said that it would be a while before you would be able to use your arm and shit. So, don't even talk to me like you gon' slip down here one night and beat they ass like you used to do them niggas back in high school and shit. You only got one arm and he got two people out in these streets that we know of looking for you. And now I'm the one sleeping on the couch, at my mama's friend's house, with my mama, brother and sister crashing or whatever as well."

"Who said I was gon' try to fight him?" Marcus said.

Those words caught Kayla's attention. Instead of randomly gazing around the way she had been for the last few minutes, she looked straight into Marcus' eyes. Did he just say what she thought he had said?

"Marcus," Kayla said. "What are you talkin' bout? What you mean you not gon' fight him? What else you gon' do?"

Marcus looked around quickly before lifting one hand up and making a gun hand gesture. Right away, Kayla's head began to shake side to side.

"What choice you think I got?" Marcus asked. "You think a nigga like this is just gon' stop cause I beat his ass and tell him to stay home or something? Hell naw. Fuck that shit. If he comin' after you and me and shit with guns and goon niggas and shit, I gotta get on his level if I wanna come out of this shit alive. He the kinda nigga that ain't gon' stop lookin' for me."

"Why don't you just give him the money for whatever was missing from what you drove up here from being down south in Texas, Marcus?" Kayla asked. "You know all that these niggas out in these streets care about is money. Why don't you just do that? Why don't you just give him the fuckin' money that he would have had for whatever was missing and call it even? Huh?"

Marcus took a moment to think of what he was going to say. He, too, had thought of doing that same thing. However, as everyone but Kayla knew at this point, the situation went much deeper than simply giving Hakim the money to match how much of the brick he is claiming was missing. If it were just that simple, Marcus would have considered doing that long before his place even got shot up and he wound up in the hospital with a bullet in his shoulder.

Marcus cringed silently, knowing that he was about to mislead Kayla yet again. There was just no way that he could tell Kayla that he smashed Hakim's chick, Tweety, when he went over to his place to drop the dude's stuff off in the garage. Marcus knew, especially at this point, that hearing something like that would probably crush Kayla even more. And she already had enough on her plate with how Hakim was targeting her as well that Marcus just did not want to add any more to her plate.

"It ain't that simple," Marcus said. "Kayla, it ain't that simple."

"Why not, Marcus?" Kayla asked, clearly tired and pushed to her limits. "Why wouldn't he just take the money? I mean, I can't live like this. This time yesterday, I was getting over to your house and we was going about our day like any other day. Now, though, you about to get on the road in a matter of minutes and head out of town while my family is basically on the run like we some damn Jews during the Holocaust or some shit. I can't even believe this shit. This is crazy."

Marcus was man enough to admit that seeing his girl stressed to this point almost made him want to cry. For the first time in his life, he knew what it meant when people said that their heart hurt. It was almost like he could feel the machinery in his heart and soul starting to squeak the more and more he thought about what his actions had caused. He wanted to say anything that would help Kayla too feel alright – anything that would help Kayla to sleep better at night. However, he knew that there was nothing that he could really say.

"I fucked up," Marcus said. He turned and looked out at the intersection. Cars swooshed down 38th Street, in both directions. For the first time in a couple of days, the skies were clear and sunny. No snowflakes fell from the sky. So much, at that very moment, Marcus wanted to tell Kayla that she should come with him. However, he knew that there was no way that she was going to leave her family. "I'm so sorry, Kayla," Marcus said, from the bottom of his heart. "I swear to God, a nigga is so fuckin' sorry."

"It's okay," Kayla said, forcing a smile. "What's done is done, ain't it? Right?"

Marcus nodded. He knew what Kayla meant, but it didn't change how he saw the situation – the situation that he had caused. "Yeah," he said. "Yeah, you right. But what you and your family gon' do? How long your mama friend gon' let all of y'all stay there, at her house, like that?"

Kayla shrugged. "I don't know," she answered. "I was thinkin' the very same thing myself when I woke up this morning to get Latrell and Linell ready for school. They wound up not goin, no way. When we rushed out of the house last night after them two niggas left, we didn't even think about how we didn't pack no clothes. So, we gon' have to go back to the house later on today or something to get some shit to just survive."

"Fuck," Marcus said. "Be careful when y'all go back over there. You never know. This nigga Hakim just might have his dudes looking for you to come back home, but I doubt it. They not gon' be doin' all that when they really want me."

"Well," Kayla said. "I thought the same thing too, but here we are. I'm the one who is out of a home for a while. And you know I been gettin' into a routine with taking Latrell and Linell to school in the morning. Oh well now, though."

"I swear," Marcus said, now rubbing his chin as he thought about what he was going to say. Hearing all of this only made him angrier. Hakim was going too fucking far over something that did not even have to do with Kayla. "I'mma kill that nigga."

"No, Marcus," Kayla said. "Don't go doin' nothin' stupid that is only gon' make shit worse."

"Make shit worse?" Marcus asked, acting as if he had just heard something crazy. "How can shit get any worse? The two of us in coffins is the only way I can see shit gettin' worse." He looked around for a brief moment, to see who was around him before he leaned in and spoke in a softer tone. "I don't know why you think I'm playin'," he said. "Just cause I got a cast and shit on my arm don't mean that I'mma just sit around and wait on somebody to come along and fuckin' kill me and shit. I'm tellin you…talkin' to this nigga Hakim ain't gon' do shit. I'mma have to kill this nigga. He just that type to where he ain't gon let shit go."

"Yeah," Kayla said. "Whatever. We will figure out what we gon' do. It's not like what we do is gonna change anything that you do, Marcus. You get to get away from all of this."

"Look," Marcus said, now coming across as a little angry. "You know this shit was my mama idea…to have me goin' up to Fort Wayne to stay with my cousin Larry for a while. You know my family and shit. And you know who I know in my family and shit. Me and Larry cool and shit, but I don't really know that nigga like that. Beyond talkin' at family reunions and when he come to town and the family be over at my mama house, I don't really fuck with him like that. He do some kind of real estate shit or somethin', that's all I really know about this. My mama think that she just gon' put me up there and I'mma just sit, but I'mma do some shit about this. I just gotta get my plan in order and stuff."

Kayla slid out of the booth.

"Where you goin?" Marcus asked, looking confused.

"Nigga," Kayla said. "You talkin' crazy and shit, like you really gon' do something from all the way up there, with no car, and your arm and shit in a fuckin' sling or cast or whatever. I'm the one down here that is basically a sitting duck."

"I know that," Marcus said, grabbing Kayla's arm gently. "Sit back down." He looked at the time on his phone. "We got like thirty more minutes before my mama come back. She went down the street to some store or somethin'."

Kayla, feeling deep in her emotions, sat back down. She rationed with herself and decided that with all that she and Marcus had been through. Plus, she could not deny the anguish that she saw in Marcus' eyes. It was too much for a young woman to see and not think that he really meant every word that he was saying. She reached back across the table and held his hands.

"Marcus," Kayla said. "It's gon' be okay."

"Yeah," Marcus said. "It's just…just…I love you so much. I almost couldn't sleep last night because I was so busy thinkin' bout what I woulda did if somethin' would have happened to you yesterday when they started shooting up my apartment."

"Don't think about the *if* about all of this, Marcus," Kayla said, trying to reinforce what little positive thinking there could be in this situation. "We can't worry about the if. And I love you too. I swear, I'mma find a way to come up to Fort Wayne and see you while you up there, for however long you up there."

Marcus smiled, liking that he for once he had a chick that he really felt was down for him and whatever he was going through. That was becoming harder and harder to find, Marcus could tell, judging by see what his boys went through with their love lives. Finding a loyal chick was becoming harder and harder to do. "We got to now, though," Marcus said. "We gotta worry about the if. We got to. That's why I said to you that you gotta be careful when y'all go back to your house and shit. I know my uncle and my boys Juan and Brandon gon' be try'na do all they can…whatever they can…to stop this shit from gettin' any worse. I need to call my Uncle Roy now that I think about it. I know he prolly worried about a nigga and shit, wonderin' why he ain't heard from me."

"I know we gotta worry about that," Kayla said. "But, like you said, your boys and your uncle gon' do something, at least something, about this shit. So, that's something. Plus, I think my mama was tired of staying over there anyway. For all I know, she might just use this as a reason to move out and get a different, nicer place or somethin'. But we gon' have to go over there sometime today or tonight to get some clothes."

"Okay," Marcus said. "Just please be careful when you do go over there. You know how some of these niggas are. They will let you think that everything is okay and everything has died down. Next thing you know, they at your door and up in your face and shit."

"I partially blame myself for some of what happened last night," Kayla said. "That's why I couldn't help but to stay up thinking about that stuff last night. Plus, I can tell that that is what my mama be thinking just by the way that she be lookin' at me. I can see it in her eyes that she wants to come out and blame me so bad for a lot of this, but it's like she just won't bring herself to say the words."

"What make you say that?" Marcus asked. "I mean, what make you say that you blame yourself for some of that shit that happened last night? Don't you start to blame yourself for any of this shit. It all is my fault and I know it and I'mma do what I can to make it better like I said."

"I know, Marcus," Kayla said. "I know. But I feel like I blame myself because, like I told y'all up at the hospital, when I went back home to help Latrell and Linell, they came back into the house and told me that two niggas came by asking if you was there."

Marcus nodded. "Yeah," he said, knowing where this was going. He decided to go ahead and let Kayla express herself and say what she was going to say. "But what that gotta do with you feeling guilty about them coming to hold your family hostage and stuff?"

"Cause, Marcus," Kayla said. "I thought about it but didn't think about it enough to think to tell my mama that two niggas came by and asked for you. When she found out–"

"You told her that?" Marcus asked.

"I mean," Kayla said, her shoulders shrugging. "It came up. And when she found out, she basically went off. I won't forget last night when the two dudes left to go to the hospital, my momma was holdin' the ice rag up to the side of her head. I could see the rage in her eyes when she found that out, and she asked me why I ain't say nothin' to her so that she could know to protect her children and shit. Next thing you know, they bustin' in the door."

"Damn," Marcus said. "I mean, don't beat yourself up about it. You were under a lot of stress from just bein' in the house when they came and shot my shit up, so don't think too bad about that."

"Yeah," Kayla said. "But I made it worse when I was takin' you home. I was ignorin' my mama callin' me, and you know she brought that up." A tear dripped out of one of Kayla's eyes then down the side of her face. She wiped her face as she continued talking. "I shoulda answered the phone," she said. "I shoulda answered the phone. She was callin' me over and over again to tell me, or ask me, where you was and stuff, and I ignored her and my brother and sister while they was over there suffering at the hands of a couple of niggas with guns and shit. I shoulda answered the phone. I can't believe I did that"

Finally, a steady stream of tears began to roll down Kayla's cheeks. Immediately, Marcus jumped up and walked over to the condiment stand in the middle of the restaurant. He grabbed a handful of napkins and brought them back over to the table. Kayla grabbed one and began to wipe the side of her face.

"Kayla" Marcus said. "You can't blame yourself. You ain't know that that was goin' on. You ain't know."

"I know I didn't know," Kayla said. "But still…but still."

Kayla and Marcus sat across from one another in the White Castle, with Marcus eventually going up to the counter to get her something to eat before his mother pulled up. Time seemed to fly by, for the both of them, as they both knew and thought that it would be the last time for a while that they would be seeing one another. By the time Kayla finished eating, the two of them could look out of the window and see Marcus' mother pulling back into the parking lot. Kayla turned away from the window and back to Marcus, knowing exactly what seeing that car meant.

"Well," Kayla said. "You gotta go now, Marcus. Your mama is pullin' up."

"Yeah," Marcus said.

The two of them slid out of the booth and dropped their trash into a trash bin near the restaurant door. They wound up going out of the door on the opposite side of the building from where Lorna had pulled into the parking lot. As soon as they stepped outside, the cold winter wind hit the both of them like a train. Instantly, Marcus pulled Kayla close to him as they both turned their backs to their wind. In so many ways, this wind was a representative of what was going on in both of their lives right then. They were truly up against the wind.

"So," Kayla asked, as the two of them walked along the side of the building, toward the front. "How long is it going to take y'all to get up to Fort Wayne? Do you know?"

"I think like two hours," Marcus said. "Maybe two hours and some change. Don't worry, though. I'mma send you a text, or call you, when I get up there to my cousin's house. I prolly text you on the way. You know ain't shit to look at between Nap and Fort Wayne."

"Yeah," Kayla said.

The two of them now came to the corner of the building. The sun shined down on them as they turned and faced one another. Kayla sniffled, causing Marcus to lightly grab her chin and hold it up to where she now looked into his eyes.

"Kayla," Marcus said, in a very serious tone. "You know I love you, Kayla. You know I love you."

Kayla looked at Marcus, into his eyes. She loved how she could look into his eyes and see the young man that she had always known. He was always so sincere – so faithful to what the two of them had. It was all too unreal right at that moment that he would be going out of town for a while. In fact, for Kayla, it almost seemed worse that Marcus was leaving than what was going on with her family.

"I love you too," Kayla said.

Marcus kissed Kayla, holding her close to him for a long embrace. Several seconds into the kiss, the two of them heard a horn beep – a horn beep that was clearly meant for the two of them. Instantly, they broke their kiss and looked in the direction where the horn had come from. Kayla saw it was Miss Lorna. Lorna waved in her rearview mirror, prompting Kayla to respond with a wave and a smile.

"You sure you don't wanna ask my mama if you can ride up north with me and she bring you back or something?" Marcus asked, looking at his mother's car then to Kayla. "I mean, I think my mama would be alright with that. Plus, it would give us more time together and shit, you know?"

Kayla nodded. "Yeah," she said. Her head then began to shake as she thought about it. As nice as doing something like that sounded to her at that moment, she knew that if she left her family vulnerable again, something else could very well pop off again. And she already had enough on her conscious that she did not want to make things any worse.

"I would," Kayla said. "But I can't go, Marcus. You know that. I can't go. I can't leave my family. My mother would never let me live again if I did. Plus, Latrell and Linell. You know they need me. If it was not for them, then maybe I would go with you and stuff, maybe even to Atlanta, but I can't leave them…not with them niggas out here and they might be after us. I just can't do that."

"I feel you," Marcus said. He wrapped his hands around Kayla's waist, wanting to feel her body against his one more time. He snickered as he thought about how he was going to miss digging in her pussy the way he had nearly 24 hours ago at this point. Oh how things can change so quickly.

"What's so funny?" Kayla asked, noticing that Marcus snickered when he grabbed her waist. "What you laughin' at?"

"How much I love you," Marcus said. He kissed the side of her head. "You know this ain't over. I know you don't believe me, but we gon' get together and I'mma handle this shit before this nigga Hakim, or his niggas, run up on me and put a bullet in my head or somethin' this time. I ain't just gon' wait. I'mma do something."

"Well," Kayla said. "Just focus on doin' one thing at a time. You goin' to Fort Wayne. Just worry about that."

Just then, Lorna tapped her horn again. Marcus and Kayla both noticed. Marcus waved at his mother's car, yelling, "I'm comin', I'm comin!"

"My mama ready to go," Marcus said.

A tear rolled down the side of Kayla's face. However, she quickly wiped it away. She knew that she had to be strong, even if she felt like breaking down and crying right there on the sideway – right there on the side of the White Castles' building. "Yeah, you better go now," she said. "Plus, it might be snowin' again later on or something and I know your mama ain't gon' wanna have to drive back in the snow."

"You want us to drop you back off at your mama's friend house?" Marcus asked.

Kayla paused and thought about it for a moment. While takeing him up on that offer would be nice, she knew that she had to be smart about some things at this point. She trusted Marcus with all of her heart, but if she was truly going to hide out from whoever he had pissed off, the fewer people that knew where she and her family was staying, the better.

Kayla shook her head. "Naw," she answered. "I mean, I would, but it's only a couple of blocks down the street." She pointed south on Keystone Avenue. "And plus, I want to walk. I need to think for a second before I go back in that house. You know how my mama is. You know how she be actin' one way one minute, and another the next."

"Did you tell her you was comin' up here to meet with a nigga before he leave and shit or naw?" Marcus asked.

Kayla shook her head. "Naw," she answered. "She already feelin' some kind of way about all of this shit, anyway. When I left out, I just told her I was goin' up to the store to get some things. Guess I betta stop at the store and get some shit so she don't think nothin' of it."

"Awe, okay," Marcus said. Even for a man, he could feel his heart hurting. He was about to be two to three hours away from his woman. He never thought something like that would happen. "Well," he said, hesitantly. "Guess I betta go on now before my mama come rollin' over here."

Kayla smiled, knowing how much she liked Miss Lorna. "Yeah," she said. The two of them kissed one last time. "You betta text me when you get up there."

"You know a nigga is gon' text you," Marcus said. "I'mma be back down here. You just watch your back. I'mma text you and tell you anything I'm doin', cause this Hakim nigga gotta be stopped. I need to hit my uncle up and see what he say. I already know my boys Brandon and Juan wonderin' why they ain't heard from a nigga, but I ain't worried about them. You my main priority."

Kayla smiled. "Okay."

The two of them kissed briefly before parting, Kayla walking toward the sidewalk along the street and Marcus walking out into the parking lot toward his mother's car. Their eyes stayed locked to the others until Marcus got into the car and put on his seatbelt. He looked at his mother.

"Aight," Marcus said. "I'm ready."

"Marcus," Lorna said. "It's cold out here. You didn't ask Kayla if she wanted us to drop her off wherever she is staying?"

Marcus nodded. "I did," he told her. "But she said that she wanted to walk to get some stuff off of her mind and stuff, you know. I did ask her, but she just wants to walk."

Lorna nodded, knowing deep down what Kayla's real reason could be for wanting to walk instead of having a ride. She knew that if she were Kayla, she would not want Marcus to know where she was staying either, especially since they were running from people. However, Lorna decided to not say anything about that part. Rather, she kept her mouth closed, backed out of the parking lot, and headed toward the parking lot exit. As she turned onto 38th Street to head toward the interstate, Marcus looked back at Kayla, who was now waiting at the intersection to cross. He kept his eyes locked on her until the intersection was too far in the distance. Once it was, he pushed his head back into the seat rest and took a deep breath. *I done really fucked up now*, Marcus thought to himself. *I done really fucked up now.*

***

Usually, Kayla would feel some kind of way about having to even walk ten feet in the snow. However, today was different. While it was probably the coldest day she had experienced for the entire winter so far, the very last thing on her mind was the cold wind. She had watched Marcus get into his mother's car and essentially roll away from her very eyes. She tried to pretend to be strong, but she knew that she was breaking down inside. As she walked back to her Godmother Lyesha's house, she did not even bother going into a store to get anything. As she crossed the intersection then up onto the snow-covered sidewalks, she knew that no matter what she bought at a store, there was no way that she would possibly be able to justify being gone for what now seemed like a good hour. She would just have to deal with whatever questions her mother had for her when she walked in the door at this point. It was not like her answers would change anything at this point, and she knew that she did not tell Marcus exactly where she was staying.

Kayla's mind was going crazy as she walked down Keystone. At first, she replayed everything that had happened over in her mind. Once those thoughts had run their course, she began to think about what Marcus had told her. She knew that his going to Fort Wayne was indeed his mother's idea. However, she also knew now that he was very serious about doing whatever he had to do to get the Hakim nigga off of his and their backs. She looked up at the sky, almost praying to God that whatever he did worked because her life was turning out to be far scarier than she had ever imagined it would be.

When Kayla walked up to Lyesha's door and knocked, the house was silent. She knew that her mother, after what happened to her last night, would not be one to jump up to answer the door quickly. Kayla knocked again.

"Mama, it's me!" Kayla announced, knocking on the door even harder. Within seconds, the door swung open and Kayla stepped into the living room that was now her home for the time being.

"Damn, girl," Rolanda said. "I was comin' to let you in."

Kayla pushed the door closed and locked it, then slid out of her coat. She tossed it onto the couch as she herself plopped down. Within seconds, she could feel her mother's eyes on her. Rolanda sat across from her daughter, on the very same couch where she had slept during the night. She looked at Kayla, noticing that she was not carrying any bags when she came walking through the door.

"So," Rolanda said. "How was the store?"

Kayla lightly cringed, not being surprised that that particular question came up. "They ain't have what I went there to get," she answered.

"Hmm, hmm," Rolanda said. "Girl, you know I wasn't born no damn yesterday or nothin'. I know your ass ain't go to no damn store. And if you did, it would not have taken you no hour and something to figure out that one of these small stores up and around her ain't have what you went there to get. Girl, why you got to lie?"

Kayla was silent. She rubbed her forehead. "I can't believe all this," she said. "It's all my fault."

Rolanda, feeling her heart soften, could pick up on her daughter's emotions right away. While she had been furious with her daughter last night, she could not feel the same after sleeping through the night. It was very clear that Kayla was the most distraught of anyone.

"Why you say that?" Rolanda asked.

"Cause, Mama," Kayla answered. "This all my fault cause I ain't think to tell you that them two dudes had come by the house and was asking Latrell and Linell if Marcus was there. I shoulda said something and maybe we would not be in this messed up situation. I shoulda said something."

"Yeah, you should have," Rolanda said. "But you can't worry about all of that now. You young and you learned...we learned...the hard way. We gotta look ahead now. We can't worry about shit that we can't do nothin' about at this point."

"Yeah," Kayla said. She knew that what her mother was saying to her was the truth. However, it would do so little to change how she was feeling. Her feelings were everywhere at the moment; her heart in several little pieces, practically rattling around in her chest.

"So, where you go?" Rolanda asked.

Kayla hesitated to answer. Really, she was thinking of what she could say that would not make her mother mad. After so many seconds, Rolanda could hear her daughter's silence.

"Kayla?" Rolanda asked. "Did you go see that boy? Y'all meet up somewhere before he leave to go wherever he going?"

Kayla nodded and answered, softly, "Yeah."

Rolanda shrugged. "I figured," she said.

"Yeah," Kayla said, somewhat surprised that her mother did not try to turn her answer into some sort of argument. "He headed up north right now, with his mama. So..."

"Well," Rolanda said. "Just worry about yourself for right now, Kayla. That's all I can really tell you. That's how life is sometime. You just got to worry about yourself and move on and learn something from all of this. Wait a minute, you ain't tell that nigga where we stayin', did you Kayla? We supposed to be hidin' and I don't need nobody to come and do harm to me and my kids again."

"No," Kayla said, shaking her head. "I ain't tell him. I don't know if he would tell his friends or what, so I figured I would just say the area and not actually where. He asked me if he wanted his mama to drop me off when she was pullin' up, but I told him no because of that that."

"Awe," Rolanda said. "Okay, then."

"So," Kayla said. "Have you talked to Lyesha? Did she say how long we could stay here or whatever? I mean...have y'all even talked about it?"

Rolanda looked away from her daughter, and down toward the floor. She shrugged as she picked up her phone and looked at it. "I texted her when I knew she would have gotten to work and stuff," Rolanda said. "But she ain't respond or nothin'."

"I see," Kayla said. "Okay."

"But I ain't try'na out stay our welcome," Rolanda said. "We definitely gon' have to find somewhere that can be a little more long term, Kayla. We gon' have to do something."

"Well," Kayla said. "I was thinking earlier, and when I was walkin' back up here from seeing Marcus. When was you try'na go back to the house to get clothes and stuff? I don't think Latrell and Linell can miss no more school. We gon' have to go back and get some more stuff since we didn't even think about that when we left."

"Yeah," Rolanda said. "I was thinkin' the same thing earlier, when you was gone and shit. We are gon' have to go back. I was thinkin' we go back tonight when they here goin' to sleep and just pack up a couple of suitcases or something."

"Yeah," Kayla said, shaking her head. "But I ain't think that we should go back at night. I feel like if these dudes really are serious about coming back after us and stuff because I told them that Marcus was in the hospital when he really wasn't, they would probably come back at night when less people would see them. That's why I was thinkin' that we should go back soon, like this morning or sometime in the middle of the day when they probably won't be rolling through and looking for us."

Rolanda nodded, thinking about what her daughter was saying. "Yeah," she said. "Maybe we all can get together and head over there in a little bit. Now that I think about it, it would be better to do some shit like that instead of goin' up in there at night. I talked to the landlord."

"What he have to say?" Kayla asked.

"You already know," Rolanda said. "That white man has just been itchin' to get us up out of there since the day we moved in and he saw a strong black woman with three kids. You know how they can be sometimes, always try'na discriminate and shit against other people. He basically said everything to me short of cussin' me out, and he just might do that when it come time to pay the rent for next month cause your mama might turn up being a little short now that I think about it. Latrell and Linell daddy betta not be late with that child support…not this month. Ain't got time for that. Anyway, Mister Ruby said that he was gon' go over and fix the back door so at least when we did come back, we ain't gotta worry about somebody sittin' up in the house and waitin' on our asses and shit. Definitely don't need no shit like that happening. Now, whether or not he done been over there to do all that, I don't know. I guess we just gon have to see, cause I ain't callin' his ass back for nothin' unless I really have to."

"I see," Kayla said. "So, when you want to head over to the house? I personally think the sooner, the better."

Rolanda looked at the time on her watch again. "Let me see what Latrell and Linell are upstairs doin'," she answered. "And maybe we can go now or something."

Chapter 2

When Brandon woke up that morning, around 11 o'clock, the first thing he thought about was his boy Marcus. He and Juan, when they got into the house last night after coming from Roy's place, had both said to one another that they thought it was funny that they had not heard from their boy Marcus yet. The first thing he did after he took his morning piss was text Marcus. He still had not gotten an answer, however.

"What time you go into work today?" Juan asked, stepping out of his bedroom. He stood in the hall and looked into Brandon's room.

Brandon, who was still lying in bed, shrugged his shoulders. "I think I go in eight, but fuck it...I ain't sure," he said. "But if we find out more about this Hakim nigga and where we can get his ass, fuck that job."

"You really think Roy is gon' go after that nigga Hakim and get him before he get Marcus?" Juan asked.

"What the fuck you mean?" Brandon asked, rhetorically. "He is gon' have to, or else. You heard what Terrell said abut Hakim, and plus what Roy and his buddy, whatever dude's name was, from last night said. It sounds like this Hakim nigga is really gon' fuck Marcus up. I can't believe Marcus smashed his chick like that, though."

"Yeah," Juan said. "I text him earlier, when I first woke up, but ain't got no response from him yet. I figured he just sleepin' in, though. I don't know what kinda shit they give you when a nigga get shot in the shoulder, but I imagine whatever they give you would make you sleep good."

"Yeah," Brandon said. "I was thinkin' the same thing."

"Cameron and Quantez hit me up just now," Juan said. "That's why I was askin' what time you was goin' into work."

"Oh, yeah?" Brandon said. "What they talkin' bout?"

"Shit," Juan said. "They was just try'na see if we wanted to chill and smoke for a minute is all. I think Quantez go into work at like four or somethin', so that's why I was askin' you."

"Fuck yeah," Brandon said. "Tell them niggas to come over. I had thought about goin' and seein' Marcus, but since he ain't answerin', we might as well smoke and shit. Why not?"

Juan chuckled and turned around, heading back into his bedroom to get his phone. "Aight then," he said. "I'll tell'em."

On that note, Brandon slid out of bed and brushed his teeth. Within thirty minutes or so, he was letting Cameron and Quantez into the front door and the four of them were chilling in the living room while Cameron rolled a fat blunt. The smoke that he had was some that Quantez had brought with him, and it smelled so good. Juan and Brandon could practically smell it when they took their coats off and took it out for them to see.

Cameron was an old friend of Juan's, as the two of them lived next door to one another in some old projects on the west side that had been torn down years ago. They managed to stay in contact, partially because Cameron would buy from some of the same people that Brandon and Juan knew until Juan started to sell on the side himself. Quantez was what many would call just a real cool nigga. He was very laid back, known for being tall and skinny while Cameron was average height with brown eyes that girls would drop their panties for.

"So, what the fuck is up with y'all niggas?" Quantez asked. When he walked in the door and got settled, he could immediately tell that something was up with Brandon and Juan. Usually, the two dudes were the happy-go-lucky type. Today, however, they were noticeably quiet compared to their usual selves.

Juan and Brandon looked at one another. At the same time, they both thought about whether or not they should say anything about Marcus to Cameron and Quantez. After a few hesitant seconds, the two of them figured that telling Cameron and Quantez would not really make much difference. Plus, Cameron and Quantez were real niggas who had real love for

Marcus. They would want to know what happened to Marcus. And Marcus would probably want them to know as well, especially since they all had chilled together so many times in the past.

"Man," Brandon said. "You not gon' believe what happened to our boy, Marcus."

Immediately, Cameron and Quantez's attention was grabbed. Cameron was licking the blunt then checking it for holes.

"What you talkin' bout?" Cameron asked.

"Yeah," Quantez said. "What the fuck you mean we not gon' believe what happened to Marcus? What happened to the nigga? He catch a case or somethin' with these racist ass cops or somethin'?"

Brandon shook his head. "Naw," he told him. "Yesterday, his shit got shot up. Two dudes rolled up to his apartment and shot his shit up."

"Damn," Cameron said. "Is you serious, nigga? Two niggas pulled up to his place and shot his shit up?"

Juan nodded. "Yup," he said. "And got him in the shoulder."

"Naw," Quantez said. "Damn, why ain't nobody tell us that shit? We would go up to the hospital to see his ass and shit, y'all niggas know that. What hospital he in so we can go up there and see him and shit?"

Brandon shook his head. "He was in Methodist, but he out now," he answered. "They said they had to let him go because the hospital is crowded or some shit. Fuck if I know. But, man, we was up at the hospital all day yesterday when his chick came callin' and tellin' us what had just happened."

"His chick?" Cameron asked. "Kayla? He still talkin' to her thick self?"

Brandon nodded. "Yeah, nigga," he said. "You know that's his boo. He ain't gon' leave that girl."

"Shit," Quantez said, smiling. "I wouldn't leave her ass either." His head shook. "That body, nigga. That shit ain't no joke. That ass."

"Yeah, well, nigga," Juan said, wanting to have some respect for his boy. "Marcus got shot in the shoulder and shit, so he gon' be alright. He ain't gon have an arm to use for a while, but he gon' be alright, at least."

Cameron grabbed a lighter off of an end table nearby and lit the end of the blunt. "So," he said. "Do he know who shot his shit up or naw? I mean, did he see'em or what?"

Brandon nodded. "He said he saw the dudes," he said. "And he even know who sent them. A nigga name Hakim."

Cameron passed the blunt to Juan, who was sitting to his right.

"Hakim?" Cameron asked.

"Yeah," Brandon said. He then looked at Juan for a split second. "You know that nigga or what?"

Cameron shrugged. "I don't know if I know him like that," Cameron said. "I mean, I heard of him, though. I feel like I know somebody that know his ass or somethin'."

"Hold up," Quantez said. "You said Hakim?"

"Yeah," Juan said, wanting to hear what Quantez would have to say. "You think you know him or somethin'?"

Quantez looked and Cameron. "Cameron," he said. "You remember when they found that nigga floating in the canal or some shit?"

Cameron thought about it for a moment. "Now that I think about it, I think I do," he answered. "They found his body up off of Thirtieth Street or something, where that bridge crosses over the canal and them old factory buildings are right there on the side of the water?"

"Yeah," Quantez said. "That's what I'm talkin' bout. The shit was on the news. But that shit was also heavy in the street too. I remember hearin' about that shit for a while. Wasn't people sayin' that some nigga named Hakim had something to do with that shit? Like the dude fucked him over or somethin'?"

Cameron nodded then looked back at Juan and Brandon. "I think I heard that shit too," he said. "But how Marcus know Hakim? I mean, why would he have Hakim after him and shit to where he shootin' up his place?"

Just as Brandon was about to explain some of the story, Juan cut him off. He was not sure what his buddy, who was generally friendlier and more open than he, was going to say. He knew that they needed to be smart with what they said. Indianapolis was just too small for them to be having any more problems because some niggas were out running their mouths and saying shit that they should not be saying.

"We don't know," Juan said, lying. "That's what we was try'na figure out. When we was up at the hospital, Marcus really couldn't tell us what all was goin' on. You know, the detectives was comin' up in there and shit. Then, you got the doctors and nurses comin' in and out of the room."

"Yeah," Quantez said. "A nigga gotta watch what you say around them kinda people. You know they just lookin' for any reason to put a nigga in jail. I wouldn't even talk about that kinda shit while I was in the hospital, I don't give a fuck what nobody say. You keep quiet. So, how did it all happen?"

"All we know is that Marcus was at his place chillin' with his chick when bullets just started flying through the windows and shit," Juan answered. "Marcus did say that he was lookin' out the window and saw two niggas pull up in a black car and get out and just start shootin' and shit. Before he could get outta the line of fire, he was on the floor and had got a bullet in his shoulder. I forget which one, but his shit is fucked up. Ain't gon' have no arm to use for a while the doctors was sayin', but we ain't talked to the nigga today yet to see how he doin'."

"Damn," Cameron said, grabbing the blunt from Juan. "That's some fucked up shit. How he know that it was the Hakim nigga who did it, though, and not somebody else or some shit?"

Brandon shrugged, having picked up on how Juan had steered the conversation just minutes before. "That's what we try'na figure out," he answered. "I mean, maybe some shit went bad or something between the two of them, but we really don't know."

"I can't imagine that, though," Quantez said. "I mean, what would Marcus do to Hakim that would make him wanna send a couple of niggas to shoot his place up and kill him? That just don't make no sense. I can't even see how they would know each other."

"Well, why he kill the other nigga?" Brandon asked. "The one that you said they found in the canal up by Thirtieth Street? Did y'all ever hear about why that nigga got got for?"

Quantez thought about it for a second. "I don't know off the top of my head," he said. "But for some reason, I think it mighta been over some chick or something. But I don't really remember."

Brandon and Juan looked at one another, each feeling a shock of fear rush through their bodies. The very thought that Hakim would put a nigga in the canal over some chick let the two of them know right then just how serious Hakim was. The fact that Marcus had come up short on the stuff he drove up from Texas only made their feelings worse. Money, drugs, and women sound fun, but there were times in life where the three just did not mix.

"I wanted to ask y'all somethin'," Brandon said, now hitting the blunt himself.

Quantez and Cameron looked at their boy Brandon. "What?" he asked. "Wassup?"

Brandon and Juan looked at one another before they looked back to Quantez and Juan. "You know where we can get some heat?" Brandon asked.

"Some heat?" Cameron asked. "Y'all niggas runnin' scared and shit now cause Marcus done got shot up and shit?"

"Fuck naw, nigga," Brandon said. "We ain't runnin' scared, and never will. We just try'na be prepared and shit incase this Hakim nigga try to do something stupid and come after us cause we friends with Marcus or something."

"I feel you on that," Cameron said. "Niggas nowadays is crazy and will do some shit like that."

"Right," Brandon said.

Last night, after Brandon and Juan had come back to their place from talking to Roy, they talked about the idea of getting a little protection. Well, Juan saw it as protection while Brandon saw it more as something they might need. If shit heated up with Roy over his nephew, the two of them knew that Roy would really appreciate having a little back up. This was especially true if this Hakim nigga was as ruthless and cold as everybody seemed to be saying.

"Well," Cameron said. "Yeah, we know some niggas that we can talk to about gettin' you some shit. It depends on how much you try'na spend and shit."

"Of course," Brandon said. "We don't care about all that, though, nigga. We just need something."

"Y'all ain't got no heat already?" Quantez asked. "I thought y'all had some shit already after all this time."

"I mean…" Brandon said. "I did, a long time ago, but when I caught that case back when, that shit went with it too."

"Yeah," Cameron said. "Well, if we hook you up with these niggas, you can't tell not one fuckin' soul where you got the shit from. I mean, no damn body."

"Nigga, you know us," Juan said. "Who the fuck we gon' tell? We don't want the police breathin' down our neck any more than you or them do, who you foolin'? You shoulda seen how quick we dipped up out that hospital when the detectives came walkin' up in there. Plus, that nigga's mama."

"Who mama?" Cameron asked. "Marcus' mama?"

"Yeah," Brandon said, rolling his eyes. "You know how that bitch be actin' when we come around. I wouldn't be surprised if she is thinkin' that she we got somethin' to do with this shit, which we don't. When we was up at the hospital, I could feel her eyes staring down the both of us like we was some criminals or some shit. We just kept our distance from her and kept it real respectful. Last thing we need is a black bitch goin' off on a couple niggas up at the hospital because she deep in her feelings or some shit."

"Yeah," Cameron said, snickering. "I feel you on that. I mean, when y'all try'na get that heat?"

Brandon and Juan looked at one another.

"Shit," Brandon said. "As soon as fuckin' possible. I mean, our boy Marcus just got shot up yesterday, so we know this shit is still fresh out here."

"Yeah," Cameron said, leaning back into the couch. "As soon as whoever did the shit find out that they ain't get Marcus, they prolly gon' try again. You know niggas will kill another nigga over any damn thing, even a pair of fuckin' Jordans and shit."

"So," Brandon said. "When you think you can hook us up with these niggas so we can get this heat as soon as fuckin' possible?"

Cameron pulled his phone out of his pocket. "I don't know," he said. "Let me hit this nigga up right now and see what he say. He stay off of Washington, out east or some shit, with his baby moms and they kids or something."

"Word," Brandon said.

The four of them passed the blunt around as they sat quietly. Cameron held his phone to the side of his face, waiting on his connect, Dre, to answer the phone.

"Sup?" Dre answered, his voice deep and smooth.

"Wassup nigga?" Cameron said. "This Cameron."

"Awe," Dre said. "Wassup wit'chu, nigga?"

"Shit," Cameron answered. "I ain't know if you was up yet, so my bad for callin' you this early in the day."

"Naw," Dre told him. "You cool. The baby moms out today, gone to her daddy house or somethin'. And she took the kids with her and shit. So, for the first time in a while, the nigga got the place to himself. And the shit feels so fuckin' nice…quiet."

Cameron snickered. "Yeah," he said, remembering the last time he had been over to Dre's apartment. There were times he could not even keep track of how many kids Dre had. When he would go over to Dre's place, all he seemed to see was a bunch of little heads running around. He could never even keep track of their names, let alone how many of them there were. "I feel you on that. But, naw, nigga, I was callin' you to see if you got that heat. I got a couple niggas who try'na get that heat."

"Man…." Dre said, sounding hesitant. "I don't know, man. You know how these streets in Nap is getting' now. All niggas wanna do now is snitch, hoping that them damn white people downtown will give them a deal or something or some shit."

"Yeah, I know," Brandon said. "But this is serious. And these are niggas that I put on everything ain't gon' give you no problem. They just need a couple guns or somethin' for a little problem they got and they asked me if I knew where to get some. I told'em I knew somebody, well a couple people, but you know I got love for a nigga, so I figured a nigga would call you first and see what you had to say and see if you can help us or not."

"Man…" Dre said. "Aight…What they try'na get? What kinda money they comin' with to try to get this heat?"

Cameron looked up at Juan and Brandon as he held the phone away from his body. "He asked what kinda money y'all comin' with," he said. "What y'all thinkin'?"

Brandon and Juan both shrugged their shoulders. "Five hundred," Brandon answered. "A thousand if we can get multiple guns."

"Aight," Cameron said. He then pulled the phone back to the side of his face. "Dre? They said they got like five hundred, but can come up off a thousand if you feel like you can let go of the right heat."

"Man…" Dre said, thinking as he spoke. "I mean, I got some shit they can take for that. Not a lot, but shit, they guns. They gon' have to be careful with one of them, though."

"Why you say that?" Cameron asked.

"Cause, nigga," Dre said, in a clearly serious tone. "One of the guns got a body on it and shit. So they gon' have to be real careful with this shit. And if they get caught with this shit and tell them racist as cops where they got the shit, I swear to God a nigga is gon' come after them."

"Nigga," Cameron said, shaking his head and smiling. "You know me. You know a nigga would not be try'na hook you up with no shady ass niggas. I don't even fuck with them kinda niggas my damn self, and you know that."

"I'm just saying," Dre said. "A nigga gotta drop in his little disclaimer, feel me?"

"I feel you," Cameron said. "But trust me, nigga. This ain't that. They just need this shit for a little problem them got and nothin' else, I swear. They ain't even gotta come in when they come get'em. If it'll make you feel better, whenever we come through, I'll be the one to come in so they ain't even gotta see you."

"Who is these niggas anyway?" Dre asked. "I know'em?"

"Now that I think about it," Cameron said. "I think y'all have met. You remember them niggas Juan and Brandon?"

"Yeah," Dre answered. "They hang out with that nigga Marcus and shit, right?"

"Exactly," Cameron said. "Them niggas. They just want a little heat and I figured there would be nobody better to ask for it then you. They was gon' go to this other nigga, but they want somebody they can trust. And that is you as far as I'm concerned."

Brandon and Juan looked at one another, knowing that what they had just heard Cameron say to Dre was a lie. However, they also knew that Cameron could be one diplomatic nigga when he needed to be. And no time was better than the present.

"Bet," Dre said. "Real recognize real, so thanks for showin' a nigga love. And them niggas cool. They practically like family to a nigga and shit. They ain't gotta wait outside or no shit like that. When they try'na come through and get this shit? The sooner the better for a nigga, personally."

Cameron looked to Juan then Brandon. "When y'all try'na go get this shit?" he asked. "He wanna know. The sooner the better, he said."

Brandon and Juan thought about it for a moment. Within seconds, the both agreed that they could get up and head over there right then.

"They said they can come right now, if you cool with that," Cameron said.

"Aight," Cameron said. "We gon head out. Me and my nigga Quantez over at they place, chillin' and smokin' and shit, so we bout to be on our way."

On that note, the two men ended the call. Immediately, Brandon and Juan got up to go get into their winter clothing.

"How cold is it outside?" Brandon asked.

"Shit," Quantez said. "Fuckin' cold. It ain't as windy as it was yesterday or nothin', but you know how this fuckin weather here is. That shit can change in a minute."

Brandon and Juan nodded as the two of them headed to the bedroom hallway and back to their bedrooms. When they both had put on pants and heavy shirts, Juan stepped into Brandon's bedroom. They could hear Quantez and Cameron talking amongst themselves out in the living room. Juan kept his voice low.

"How we gon' get the money without them seein?" Juan asked Brandon.

Brandon stopped and thought about it for a moment. "Damn," he said. "They is sittin' out in the livin' room. They can definitely see a nigga's stash from there."

"Right," Juan said, nodding his head. "That is the same exact shit I was just thinkin'."

There was a brief pause. "I know," Brandon said. "You talk to'em and shit, about whatever, I don't give a fuck what it is, and I'll get the shit real casual like to where they won't even notice what the fuck I'm doin'."

Juan thought about it for a second. "Aight," he said. He finished pulling his Timberlands over his feet. "Good idea. Make that shit quick."

Brandon grabbed his coat just as Juan was coming out of his bedroom and the two of them headed to the living room. While Juan distracted Cameron and Quantez by talking about some big booty chicks he had seen when he and Brandon were leaving the hospital from seeing Marcus, Brandon went into the kitchen. Glancing behind him every so often, he opened the freezer door and grabbed out the box of fish sticks. Quickly, but smoothly, he carried the box of fish sticks over to the counter. He pulled open the top of the box and looked inside to be sure that the money was still in their little hiding spot.

After pulling out $1,500 in one hundred dollar bills, Brandon looked over the counter to see if either Quantez or Cameron were looking in his direction. Luckily, the two of them were both moving their hands about as they described a stripper's ass that they had seen the last time that they went to the strip club. Quantez went on and on for several seconds about a beautiful dark skin chick that he had seen in Atlanta during his last time visit with an ass that "had its own orbit."

Brandon snickered as he closed the fish sticks box back up and threw it back into the freezer. To make sure he threw Quantez and Cameron off, he walked back to his bedroom for a quick second before coming back out into the living room.

"I'm ready if y'all are," Brandon said, standing near the doorway. The other three guys stood up and they headed outside. Out on the sidewalk, they wound up deciding that Brandon and Juan would get into their car and follow Cameron and Quantez out to Dre's house.

***

Dre lived in a small apartment complex on east Washington Street, not too far from an area of Indianapolis called Irvington. The complex, which consisted of only two or three buildings, was down a slope from Washington Street with the parking lot letting out to Pleasant Run at the back. After carefully sliding down the slope and into the parking lot, Brandon pulled his car into the parking spot next to Cameron.

They all stepped out of their cars at the same time and headed into the apartment and upstairs. After knocking on the door and saying who they were, Dre opened the door and the four of them shuffled inside.

"Damn," Dre said, as he shook all four of their hands. "Y'all dressed like y'all some damn Eskimos or some shit, up in Alaska or some shit."

They snickered.

"You know how niggas are," Brandon said, laughing. "You know niggas ain't with all this cold weather and shit."

"I know that's right," Dre said. He then pointed at his living room furniture as he locked the door. "Have a seat, niggas. Damn. Make yourselves comfortable and shit. We peoples and shit, right?"

Brandon and Juan looked around at Dre's apartment. While they had seen some pretty nice apartments in their lifetime, Dre definitely had his apartment decked out. The first thing they noticed was what looked like a polar bear area rug. It seemed to sprawl across the middle of the living room floor, white and fluffy. Black art hung on the walls – mostly oil paintings of old black musicians and politician from back in the day. To say the least, neither of them thought for one minute that the art they were seeing on the wall was cheap. That shit looked almost as if it were done custom, just for Dre's apartment.

Dre's furniture was practically out of the plastic new. His dining room table was some funny kind of wood that neither of them had ever seen. The four of them sat down as Dre walked back to a bedroom. He reappeared in a matter of seconds, now carrying a blunt.

"I know y'all niggas said that y'all was smokin' and shit when you called me and shit," Dre said. "But, fuck, if y'all wanna share this, we can."

Dre, who was a dark skin dude with pretty white teeth and big eyes, leaned down and handed the blunt to Cameron. He then pointed at a lighter that was setting on the coffee table. Soon enough, he was sitting across from the four of them, on a different part of the suede sectional.

"So, wassup?" Dre asked, rubbing his hands together as he watched his company get comfortable and smoke the blunt. "Y'all niggas need some heat, huh?"

Brandon and Juan glanced at one another. "Yeah," Brandon answered, taking the lead. "We don't know if we gon use the shit, but just in case we need it, you know what your mama would always tell you about umbrellas."

Dre snickered. "Yeah," he said. "It's betta to have it and need it then to need it and not have it."

"Exactly," Brandon said.

"Well, I can help y'all out with that," Dre said. "I don't know if Cameron told y'all niggas or naw, but one of the guns got a body on it. So, y'all niggas gon have to make sure that you're extra careful with this shit. And you ain't get it from me."

"Understood," Brandon said, confidently.

"Yup," Juan said. "We got'cha."

"Aight then," Dre said. "If you don't mind me askin', what kinda problem y'all got to where y'all feelin' like y'all need to have some heat?"

"This nigga," Brandon said, shaking his head. "Well, a couple niggas, actually, if you wanna get technical with it. I don't know if you heard or not, but our boy Marcus got shot up."

"Huh?" Dre said, genuinely surprised. "Who shot Marcus up? When? Where?"

"His place," Brandon answered. "And it all happened yesterday. We was up at the hospital yesterday, all day and shit, until the detective and shit came." Brandon knew that since he did not know Dre all that well, he would need to be careful with what he said when talking to him. You just cannot trust too many niggas, he thought. "Marcus told us that two dudes pulled up and just shot up his shit," Brandon said. "He got hit in the shoulder and shit and had to go to the hospital and shit, but he gon' be okay."

"Glad to hear that," Dre said, shaking his head. "Who did it? Who shot his shit up? Or, do he even know it was?"

"Naw," Brandon said, shaking his head. "He don't know yet. Well, he ain't figured it out. That's why we need this heat, feel me? Since we don't know who did this shit, we need to be prepared in case these crazy ass niggas come after us or something because we friends with his ass or something."

"Yeah," Dre said, shaking his head. "You can never be too careful. That's why my chick went downtown and got her shit legit. And we stay strapped up. Cause you never know when some crazy nigga is gon' get bold enough to run up in your shit and try to do you and yours some harm." Just then, Dre pulled a gun out from under the couch cushion. "That's why you gotta stay ready just in case, feel me?"

Brandon and Juan smiled. "Yeah," Juan said, handing the blunt to Brandon. "That's exactly what we sayin'. Since we don't know who these niggas are, or if they gon' come back and try again or come after us or some shit, we just need something just in case."

"Aight," Dre said nodding his head. "I can feel a nigga on that. Ain't nothin' wrong with that. It's good you thinkin' and shit, cause a lotta niggas don't…until some shit done happen to they ass and they saying coulda, woulda, shoulda and all that shit."

"Right," Brandon said.

"Aight," Dre said, standing up. "I'll be right back."

Just then, Dre walked back to his master bedroom. He rumbled around in his closet, moving bins and boxes out of the way. Soon enough, he had pulled out a big green plastic box. He popped the top off and leaned down onto one knee while he played around with the safe combination. Soon enough, the safe was open. He moved stacks of money out of the way and pulled up two glocks. He smiled as he looked at them. Part of him could not believe that he was going to part with them. However, he also figured that he would be better of getting rid of them than he was getting caught with them. Quickly, he put the closet back together in just the same way it had been before he got the safe out. He glanced down the bedroom hallway to make sure that some of his company was not walking up on him. When he saw that they were not, he finished and carried the guns out to the living room.

Immediately, Juan and Brandon's eyes were drawn to the black guns in Dre's hands. They glanced at one another, knowing that shit was starting to get real now. Immediately, Brandon felt a little pride. He knew that Roy would be proud that Marcus' boys were actually doing something about what happened to his nephew. That would get them so much respect.

Dre handed one gun to Juan then the other to Brandon.

"This the shit I was tellin' y'all bout," Dre said.

Juan looked over the gun, feeling how heavy the metal felt in his hands. "Damn," he said, loving the feeling of power in his hands. "This shit fire hard and shit?"

Dre smiled, sitting back down. "Fuck yeah," he answered. "Them ain't the biggest guns in the world or nothin', but a nigga is definitely gon' feel his shoulder snap back when he fire that shit. And all you gotta do is fire once and the nigga is out like a fuckin' crashed race car in the fucking Five Hundred or some shit."

Everybody snickered.

"How much you want for each?" Brandon asked, pushing his hands into his pockets.

Dre looked at both Brandon and Juan and the guns that he had just handed them. "Give a nigga three hundred for each," he said. "And we call that shit a deal."

"Aight," Brandon said, nodding his head. He liked the price, and he liked that he was working with a nigga that he could trust.

"But remember what I told y'all niggas," Dre said. "Y'all ain't get that shit from me."

"We got you," Brandon said, smiling. He handed six one hundred dollar bills across the room to Dre. "Here you go."

"Thank you," Dre said, then began to count the money. "So, y'all don't know what Marcus done got caught up in that would cause somebody to be out try'na put a bullet in his head?"

Brandon shrugged. "Yes and no," he answered.

"They said that that nigga done got hooked up with Hakim or some shit," Quantez said. "You know Hakim, don't you? That nigga that had something to do with that one nigga they found floatin' in the damn canal and shit over on the west side."

"Hakim?" Dre asked, just as he finished counting the money. His eyes were practically bugged out of his face, letting everybody in the room know just how surprised he was at what he had just heard. "Marcus in some shit with that nigga?"

Brandon and Juan looked at one another. Yet again, the plot seemed to only be thickening for their boy Marcus. The look on Dre's face said it all.

Chapter 3

The further away from Indianapolis Marcus got with his mother, the more he thought about how much he wanted to get the hell out of Indiana. He looked around at the farmland that hugged both sides of Interstate 69 and shook his head. He knew that he was not going to be in some old country town or anything like that, but the fact that he was seeing all this space only made him think even more.

While his mother played her 90s rap music as she drove the car, Marcus looked down at his cell phone. He saw that his boys Juan and Brandon had both text messaged him earlier in the morning. At first, he started to respond to their messages, but decided that he would need some more time to figure out what he was going to say. As much as he wanted to tell his boys that he was going up to Fort Wayne to lay low with his cousin for a while, he remembered what his mother had said. It truly was probably a better idea that he just kept that bit of information to himself. However, he could not help but to feel like he was not being a real nigga by doing that.

Instead of responding to the text messages, he looked at the last time he was texting his uncle, Roy, and replied: wassup.

After several minutes, he noticed that Roy was not responding as quickly as he normally would. He wondered why, almost to the point where he wanted to simply put the phone up to the side of his face and call. However, he knew that his mother would probably say something. And the last thing he felt like dealing with right then was hearing his mother go on and on the way she would do something.

Once again, it must have been like Lorna was reading her son's mind.

"You're not texting them two so called friends of yours, are you Marcus?" Lorna asked, looking over at her son.

Marcus shook his head. "Naw, Mama," he said. "I remember what you said and shi—stuff. I ain't gon text them. They text me, but I ain't respond."

"Marcus," Lorna said. "I'm telling you, baby. I know you grown and think you know everything, but sometimes it is just better to not say anything at all, especially when you don't know what is going on."

"I know, I know," Marcus said. "I actually was just textin' Uncle Roy, but, for some reason, he ain't respondin'."

Lorna started to open her mouth to say something, but decided against it. She knew how close Marcus had always been to her brother Roy. However, she also knew that such very closeness was part of the reason that he was caught up in the predicament that he was in now. Instead, she just shook her head while looking ahead at the interstate.

"He is probably busy, Marcus," Lorna said. "You just worry about you right now. I called your cousin Larry right when I pulled up at the White Castles to pick you up and stuff. I just hope that we don't run into any traffic on the way up here cause he said that he would only have so long to leave work to come let you in."

"I see," Marcus said, not being all the enthusiastic about going to stay with his cousin.

"Marcus," Lorna said. "I want you to really make this work out for you, in a good way. You hear me? I do not want you up here, in Fort Wayne, making friends with the same kind of people that you were friends with back in Indianapolis."

"Mama," Marcus said. "Fort Wayne ain't got all that goin' on like that."

"Oh yes it does, Marcus," Lorna snapped back. "It may not be as big as Indianapolis is and whatnot, but you have got to remember that it is on the way to Detroit. Stuff goes down up her just like it does in Indianapolis…just like it does everywhere. That is why it is up to you to watch who you associate with so you don't make your situation even worse…so you don't have more than one situation going at a time."

"I got it, Mama," Marcus said, looking out at the side of the road. Just then, he felt his phone vibrate. He looked down and saw that it was a text from Kayla: Hey.

Marcus held his phone up. "Kayla textin' me now," he said, out loud to his mother.

"I really do feel for that girl, Marcus," Lorna said. "I really hope that her family is not affected by this mess any more than they already are. I swear, I was up thinking about that last night. And I can only imagine if I were in their place."

Marcus zoned out on what his mother was saying to him. Instead, he could only really focus on his text message conversation with Kayla.

Kayla: Wyd

Marcus: On this fuckin road. Wyd

Kayla: Me and my mama about to go over to the house to get some stuff

Marcus: Oh

Kayla: Yeah

Marcus: Just be careful, Kayla. Okay?"

Kayla: I will, I will.

Marcus zoned back in to his mother talking as he looked up at the road, waiting on a response text from Kayla to pop up.

"Remember what I told you, Marcus," Lorna said to her son. "Please, remember what I told you." All the while, Lorna reminded her son of what he would need to do to hopefully get out of this situation alive. She thought about her brother Roy. She was not sure what her brother really had in store to try to help his nephew out of this situation. However, she hoped that whatever he did, he would do it soon and quickly. The sooner the better was Lorna's point of view.

Lorna continued driving the car toward Fort Wayne, north on Interstate 69. Little did she know, her brother Roy was already on it, back in Indianapolis, trying to get that much closer to Hakim.

Chapter 4

Roy wound up falling straight to sleep after Cherry had given him some of that fire head that she was so good at. The two of them had basically remained in the bed, chit-chatting with one another until they dozed off. However, Roy did not sleep as long as Cherry did. When he woke back up, within a couple of hours or so, it was really because the sun was beaming so brightly into his bedroom window, almost seeming to be ten times as bright as it normally would because of the winter wonderland that was outside. Instantly, Roy looked down at Cherry's chocolate body – her killer shape barely covered by the thin white sheet that she had pulled up over her body after she had pulled her head up from Roy's lap. Within seconds, Roy was looking up at the ceiling, thinking.

Soon enough, Roy almost felt stupid for not thinking of it sooner. A nigga he knew named George, who he actually used to know quite well, would be the perfect person that he could get into contact with if he wanted to really get close to Hakim again after all these years. Even with his "chocolate bunny" lying in the bed next to him, Marcus was constantly at the back of his uncle's mind. George would be the perfect person for Roy to get in contact with because the two of them know one another fairly well. They also were the kind of dudes, especially at this point in their life, that would have a little common ground to meet up without it all being the least bit suspicious. On top of that, however, Roy knew that he would have to come up with some way to bring Hakim up in the conversation if he wanted to seem as smooth as possible for wanting to get into contact with him.

George and Roy went to the same high school together. Roy could easily recall them having a couple of classes together as well as sitting together during the lunch period for at least two or three years of high school. Shortly after high school, however, Roy's memory got a little foggy when it came to George. It seemed like he disappeared for a while, maybe after catching a case or something. Whatever the reason was, Roy could not really remember seeing George much when the two of them would have been in their early twenties. However, as they got closer to thirty years old, their paths had begun to cross again since high school. At first, the two saw one another at a BBQ for either the 4th of July or Labor Day. Roy could not really remember which one. Then, after that instance, Roy wound up going to an after party of sorts with his boys at the time where a couple of strippers were being passed around in a back room. Roy and George were not in the rooms at the same time or anything like that, but Roy could remember clearly seeing him there.

Since then, Roy would see George every so often and they always seemed to be genuinely cordial with one another. What made George the perfect person to talk to in Roy's eyes to get to Hakim is the fact that George was basically the Mister Nice guy in the hood. Everybody loved him. And most people, especially those about that life, knew him. You never heard about him getting into it with anybody, or sleeping with anybody's chick for that matter. Furthermore, he also dated some chicks over the years that were what you could call "high profile" – popular, well-liked, and good looking. On top of all that, however, his name stayed out of people's mouths. Last Roy had heard anything about George, which was just some months ago, him and some buddy of his had basically become business partners. The two of them started to flip houses together, especially buying up homes in poorer parts of town that might be coming up in the near future. Roy knew that he could call Roy about trying to talk to him about getting a house off of him or something. Nothing would seem the least bit odd about that. Now, however, he just had to look through his phone to see if he had George's phone number. He thought that he did have the number but was not sure.

Roy lay in bed for a few more minutes, feeling around on the bed to see where his phone could have gone too. When Cherry had come into the bedroom, with the look in her eyes that was telling him she really needed the dick, he could not really remember what he had done with his phone. If he had dropped it onto the bed, he knew it would definitely be harder to find it now. When Cherry came over, his bed always looked wild after he was done long stroking that ass.

Soon enough, however, Roy had felt around far enough on the bed and found his phone under the pillow. He pulled it out and slid out of the bed, careful to try to not move Cherry too much to the point where she would wake up. As he slid out of bed and looked at her, he could see that she was clearly knocked out – in la-la land. He simply pulled the sheet further over her body and closed the blinds a little more so that the room would not be so lit up as it was right then. He pulled his sweatpants back on, slid into a shirt, and headed out into the living room with his phone.

Roy sat on the couch, after checking out front of his house. After years of living in the business – a business where it is easy to have people popping up at your house unannounced – it had basically become an instinct of his to check his surroundings before getting too comfortable. He especially did this before talking business, as sometimes the walls could have ears too, or so he thought.

Roy scrolled through his phone and found that he did have Roy's phone number. At first, he was starting to do what he might normally do with the younger generation: send a text. However, he snapped out of that train of thinking. He and George were in the same age group – late thirties, early forties –, so he figured that calling instead of sending a text message just might be the way to go.

"Hello?" George answered, sounding professional.

"Hey, man," Roy said, sounding upbeat. "It's Roy, man. How you been?"

"Roy?" George said. "Roy over off of Harding, on the west side?"

Roy chuckled. "Yeah, man," he said. "That Roy. How you been, my brother?"

"Man, this is crazy," George said. "I was just thinkin' bout you, my brother, not too long ago. I think I was somewhere and I saw somebody that look like you or I thought that they was you or something."

"Awe, yeah," Roy said. "Mighta been me."

"Naw," George said. "When I got close enough, I saw it wasn't you, brother. So, man, how you been doin'? Wassup?"

"Oh, I been doin' okay," Roy said. "Can't really complain, I guess."

Roy was cool with George, but did not want to be that nigga that talked about his drug dealing life with a dude who made his money from flipping housing – from real estate activities.

"That's good," George said. "That's good. Glad to hear it."

"Yeah," Roy said. "But I was callin' you man cause I wanted to know if you was still involved in that house flipping stuff you used to be doin' back when. You still doin' that?"

George chuckled. "Yeah, man," he said. "That shit is good money."

"I bet it is," Roy said. "I'm lookin' to maybe move up out of this place I'm stayin' in over here. Maybe get me somethin' that is a little more modern or something. And when I was lookin' at some houses that had obviously been redone, I guess, that is when I thought of you and I was like, man I should call that nigga George and see what he got to say since you in that business. You got any houses that I could maybe check out. You know me, man. I ain't lookin' for no big monster house or anything, but I don't want no tiny little box either. You know, somethin' that is just right and maybe in a better part of town or something, feel me?"

"Yeah, man," George said. "I got you. Actually, it's funny that you callin' me right now and asking me about something like this because I was just getting ready to head out the door to go do some stuff at this property I got over on the southeast side, not too far from Fountain Square. What you think about that kind of neighborhood?"

Roy paused for a few seconds, making it seem like he was truly giving it some thought. "I mean," he said. "It's cool, I guess. Some parts, I should say. Depends on the street if you really wanna know, cause you know how some patches are over there. Some nice, and some not so nice."

"Yeah," George said. "You right about that. But this is one of the parts that the white folks done came through and started to redo. I got this house off of this old white lady that was about to die not too long before they came through and started to fix this neighborhood up. Only problem, though, is..."

"Awe man," Roy interjected, trying to sound genuine as he looked ahead from his couch and out the window at the street as cars slowly rolled by. "What's the problem, man? What's wrong with it?"

"Naw, man," George said, chuckling. "Ain't nothing wrong with the house, man. That ain't the problem. The problem is that they white people done came through here and started building up condos and stuff. You know, like that stuff you see downtown and shit. Futuristic, like we supposed to be Seattle or some damn where."

Roy chuckled, knowing exactly what George meant.

"Yeah, man," George said. "So the house kinda don't fit into the block any more like it used to, but if you wanna see it, you can come on by. You might like it. I can give you a good deal on it, too."

Roy nodded as he talked into the phone. "Aight then," he said. "When can I come through and see it?"

"What you doin' in about an hour or so?" George asked. "I'll be over there, like I said, I gotta do some things today and going over there to handle some business and check on some things is one of them. Man, you can come through and I can show you around a little bit if you wanna see it and I can show you what we done did to the house and what we planning to do."

"Sounds good," Roy said.

George gave Roy the address then told him that if he had problems finding the house, or the street it was on since the street never came all the way out of its neighborhood to actually intersect with any major street, that he should just call him back. Roy agreed and the two hung up. Roy now felt like he was finally getting some way with at least trying to stop what his nephew was going through. No matter what, he was not going to just sit by and watch his own younger sister lose her only child to some foolish mess. He had personally watched her struggle to raise that boy from birth, almost on her own in a lot of ways, and he was not going to watch her have to put him into the ground. Roy had seen their aunt grieve for what seemed like forever about her son being killed. And Roy did not want to see it happen again, as it was just too much to watch even from a distance.

Roy looked at the time, knowing that he had better go ahead and get some clothes on. He was not sure if it had snowed again, but going to where George's house was from where Roy lived meant taking the street way through multiple neighborhoods and downtown. The latter would surely add more time to his trip, not to mention stress if there was snow on the ground, or even ice.

Roy stood up and walked back into his bedroom. After standing in the doorway for a second, and contemplating if he wanted to bend Cherry over for a quickie before he got ready, he walked over to his dresser, pulled out some clothes and went to take a shower. Within fifteen or twenty minutes, he was just about ready to head out the door. Just as he slid into his coat, he knew that he should leave Cherry a little something – a little something that would definitely keep that ass coming back for some more of the dick. He pulled a few one hundred dollar bills out of his wallet, folded them together, then sat them on top of her purse. He told himself, in his head, that he would remind himself later on to send her a text that said she needed to be back over to his place later so he could break her off again. He hated to leave her sleeping in his bed after blowing her back out like he was still in his twenties, but this was business that he really needed to handle.

After Roy let his car warm up, he backed out of his driveway and headed toward downtown so he could get to the southeast side of town where Fountain Square is. All the while, as he drove, he went back in forth in his mind as he tried to think of ways he could bring Hakim up. He only hoped, however, that George knew Hakim as well, or half as well, as he thought he would. George's 'Mister Nice Guy' persona was just what Roy needed, because George was the kind of guy that knew everybody, in and out of the life in the streets.

***

When Roy pulled up outside of the house, he could see immediately what George had meant when he had told him on the phone that the house did not really fit in with the neighborhood as much anymore. Many of the corner buildings had been converted from red brick corner store kinds of buildings to brown brick buildings with coffee shops and bookstores on the ground floors below newly renovated apartments. As Roy drove down the street, he could see how many of the houses that were once ran down. Victorian homes were now remodeled and practically looked totally different – obviously old, but converted to four apartments or something to that affect. The house that Roy owned was definitely older, but maybe not quite as modernized as the rest of the houses on the block were. For a split second, Roy thought about moving up out of his neighborhood and changing his game up a little bit to where nobody knew where he lived like they knew now, but rather he lived over in a part of town that nobody would have suspected.

As soon as Roy was getting out of his car, he could see George walking up the street from his parked car.

"Man, I was just about to call you," George came up saying, smiling. "I was going to see if you had trouble finding it or whatever. I didn't know how well you knew the area of what."

"Naw, man," Roy said, shaking hands with and hugging the 5'8" dude. "I know my way around over here, kinda. So, this is the house, huh?" Roy pointed up toward the house with the address that he remembered George telling him. "Ain't too bad."

"Yeah," George said, the browned-skin man with jet black hair turning toward his property. "Bought this, like I told you, from some old white lady some years back, before the recession. Me and my partner been fixing it up, here and there, doing stuff while we was waiting on the economy to come back up. Once it did, the neighborhood looked different and, so, now, here we are."

Roy nodded, part of him wishing that he could be half was sociable and likeable as George was.

"Aight then," Roy said. "Well, let me see what it looks like and I gone and get out of your hair and shit."

On that note, Roy followed George into the house. The two of them chatted about this and that. George asked how Roy's sister Lorna was doing, with Roy saying that she was doing fine, leaving out Marcus altogether. After Roy had seen the three bedrooms, two baths, and open floor plan that was the first floor, the two men stood around in the front room of the house.

"Yeah, man," Roy said, after hearing the price. "I'mma definitely have to think about this." He looked around, particularly liking the white brick fireplace that was clearly brand spanking new. "This is kinda what I was lookin' for. Don't know about livin' near these white niggas over here, but still…like you said, the neighborhood has definitely been comin' up lately."

"Yeah, man," George said, nodding his head. "Yeah, just think about it. I didn't know how soon you were lookin' at maybe making the move, but me and my partner are definitely trying to get this house off of our hands. And, of course, we would rather sell it to one of our own rather than somebody else."

"I feel you on that," Roy said, liking how George still had that sense of being proud to be black – that pride that he remembered the black community having back when he was a kid. "So, do you still keep up with any of the old crew." Roy knew that he needed to name off random names that he remembered as running in some of the same circles as he and George back in the day and throughout the years. "Anybody from high school? Rick? Johnny? Hakim? Sandra?"

"Now that you mention it," George said, smiling and nodding his head. "I do, in a way. I saw Sandra not too long ago. I think I was at the Kroger up north or somewhere like that. She still look good – still got that ass that all the niggas went crazy over."

"Is that so?" Roy asked, remembering just how bad of a body Sandra had back in high school, back in the nineties. Now that he thought about it, the last time that he had seen

Sandra, she was looking pretty good too. And this was after popping out a couple of kids.

"Yeah," George said. "And I also keep in touch with Hakim, you know."

"Naw," Roy said, now hearing music to his ears. "I didn't know if you and Hakim was cool like that and stuff. I thought you was, but I wasn't really sure."

"Yeah," George said. "That nigga." His head shook. "He a fool, you know, but we still coo. I chill with him every so often, when I get a little time. I got a cousin or two that are real close to him, so they hang with him and whatnot more than I would."

"Now that I think about it," Roy said. "I was try'na get into contact with Hakim again a while back, but the number I had in my phone for him wasn't right." Roy pulled his phone out of his pocket as he told his lie. "I called it and some chick answered, saying that he wasn't there and to not call that number askin' for him no more."

George swatted his hand. "Man," he said. "You know how Hakim be, man. You know that brother keeps a woman around him, even when he deep in baby mama problems. That coulda been one of his chicks or something, in they feelings or something, and just not wanting him to make a move because they were not getting enough attention."

"Yeah," Roy said, snickering. "That's women for you. But, yeah, I was try'na reach out to him to talk to him about some stuff that's happenin' out in the streets that I think he need to know, but it ain't no big deal."

"Man," George said. "Hakim cool. I can get in touch with him and tell him that you try'na get in touch with him. I would give you his number, but you know how people are about that."

"Of course, of course," Roy said. "I know that feelin', and I ain't mad at the nigga for that either. I thought about stoppin' by his place, but I ain't wanna get shot up."

"Yeah," George said. He pulled his cell phone out of his pocket. "In fact, let me go ahead and text him right now, telling him that you want to get in touch with him. You want me to give him your number, man?"

Roy gave George his phone number, holding back a smile the entire time. While he still was not totally sure, and could not be, that Hakim would hit him back after getting a message from George, he still accomplished something. Not only did he come to look at the house, which was starting to tempt him to really think about moving, but he also at least found somebody that was really cool to get to Hakim. Now, though, he only had to wait and see what would happen. He could only hope that Hakim would hit him up, as he constantly thought about how his younger sister Lorna was taking her son up to Fort Wayne so that he could lay low for a while.

"Thanks, man," Roy said to George. "You ain't have to, but thanks man. I was just wantin' to talk to him, plus catch up and shit since he a real nigga. You know, we gettin' older and shit and just wanted to keep in touch with some people."

"Ain't nothin' wrong with that," George said. "Ain't nothin' wrong with that. I'll let you know if he responds to me or not, or you just tell me when he reach out and talk to you and stuff, so that I know or not. Hakim cool, though, man. He'll probably reach out, especially to you, real quick or something."

Roy smiled. "Yeah," he said. "But thanks for showin' me the house man." He looked around. "I'mma give this some thought and maybe hit you back up in a few days or something."

"Yeah, man," George said. "You do that. Let me know what you think about it, the price, and if it's something that you wanna buy. It'd probably be a good investment for you, but that's just my opinion."

"Naw, naw," Roy said. "You right, you right. Aight, well I'll let you go on and get done what you need to do today. Thanks again, man."

On that note, Roy stepped out of the house, leaving George inside as he got onto his cell phone and pulled papers out of a folder. Roy rubbed his hands together when the wind blew down the narrow street, like a cold tunnel, as he walked down the walkway to the sidewalk and to his car. When he got inside and pulled off, he looked inside of George's house, at him pacing around the middle of the living room floor while talking on a cell phone. He waved, not sure if George would be able to see, before he was gone and down the street.

On his way back to his place, Roy felt a little pride at how tactful he could be when he wanted to get something done. Today, in his eyes, was surely proof of that. He only hoped, at that very second, that Marcus would be smart. He could only hope that Marcus would not do anything while he was up in Fort Wayne that would make his situation any worse, like telling somebody where he was going that would be out in the streets running their mouth. From what Roy remembered about Hakim, he was just the kind of nigga who would ride right on up to Fort Wayne in the middle of the night and handle his business like a ghost and be gone and back in Indianapolis by the morning, as if nothing had ever happened.

Roy began to give some more thought to what Lorna had told him last night. While he really did want to respect his sister's wishes, especially when he considered that everything she was doing was just to try to be sure that her only child would be okay and not wind up dead, he knew that he was probably going to have to go against her. Roy knew that he would have to get in touch with his nephew, just to make sure that his head was in the right place. That would make the world of difference in what Roy was doing. Plus, Roy was also tired of hearing all of what supposedly happened second hand – tired of hearing it from Brandon or Juan or his sister Lorna. Rather, he wanted to hear it all from his nephew so that he knew every bit of what there was to know before he went through the diplomatic efforts of actually getting close to Hakim and stopping him before he put a bullet into his nephew's head.

When Roy pulled up out front of his house about twenty minutes later, he smiled. Cherry's car was still parked out front, meaning that that ass was still lying under his sheets – that that ass was still lying in his bed, taking a nap after the deep dicking just a couple of hours ago. He looked down at his lap, knowing that he was not young like he used to be. When he checked his phone and saw that Hakim had not reached out and text messaged or called him yet, he told himself that he could go at it again. To his surprise, when he walked into the house and to his bedroom, Cherry had just woken up. She motioned with her index finger, telling Roy to walk up to the bed.

"Come here, nigga," Cherry said, smiling.

Roy smiled, knowing what that meant. He walked up to the bed, just like Cherry had told him to do. He leaned over and smacked her ass, loving how she giggled when he did that. She pretended to not like it, but he knew that she did. There was no denying that. When Roy's shins were flush against the side of his bed, Cherry crawled over to his side, putting a sexy arch in her back as she did so. Roy knew that she knew exactly what she was doing to a nigga. And he was not the least bit mad that she was doing it.

Within seconds, Roy's head was rubbing the back of Cherry's head. She had unbuckled his pants, unzipped his fly, and taken his dick deep into her mouth. All the while Roy groaned as he felt and enjoyed Cherry's sexy, silky mouth, the last thing he heard was his phone vibrating. He had left his phone in his coat pocket, having left dropped his coat onto a couch when he walked through the front door.

"You like suckin' that dick?" Roy asked.

Cherry mumbled yes, her mouth and jaws too stretched for her to speak and Roy's grip too firm on the dome of her head for her to come up. Within a matter of minutes, Cherry had worked her magic. She got Roy's manhood up to full mast, sticking straight out from his body in the dimly lit atmosphere that was his somewhat cluttered bedroom.

"Turn that ass around," Roy told Cherry.

Cherry did just as she was told, turning her beautiful dark skinned body around while keeping her pretty eyes locked with Roy's eyes. As soon as her ass was up in the air and pointing at Roy, she felt his warm face pressing down between her ass checks. She smiled and squirmed, feeling him go lower and lower until his tongue ravished her pussy.

"I need this pussy, baby," Roy said. He leaned forward and down and feasted on Cherry. "This shit taste good."

Soon enough, Roy was long stroking deeply into Cherry's insides. She moaned and squired around like the deep feeling was something new to her. Roy smiled, knowing that any nigga in her age group probably could not do it like he could do it. All the while he enjoyed the depths of Cherry's pussy, he had not realized he missed a call from Hakim.

Chapter 5

After Kayla got done with texting Marcus, not really sure of what she should text him to begin with, she chilled on the couch for a moment. As much as she did not want to look around at the place that had been her bedroom the last night, it was obvious that her life had changed. As positive as she tried to think about the situation, there was something that was just real about what was going on right now. It was scary; it had happened so quickly. On top of all that, it all had blinded her. As much as she knew that she loved Marcus – and that was very much, mind you – she could not really come up with the words to text him. She knew that he was on his way up to Fort Wayne, to lay low. If only I knew somebody out of town, Kayla thought to herself as she looked across the room at her mother and brother and sister, who are were getting ready.

"Y'all make sure you zip your coats up far enough," Rolanda said, authoritatively to Latrell and Linell. "I ain't been outside since last night, so I don't know what the weather is like. Or that wind for that matter. Just make sure y'all zip y'all shit up. The last thing I need right now is one of y'all getting' sick while we stayin' here."

Kayla, noticing that her mother had begun to pat the wound on the side of her head, snapped out of her daze for a moment. She had been sitting in her coat, thinking about how Marcus was leaving the city so much that she had not really been helping her younger brother and sister get ready. They were headed over to the house so they could get their things. Kayla stepped over to Latrell and Linell and helped them to get all of the way into their coats.

"You want me to drive, Kayla?" Rolanda asked. "Or do you think that you'll be okay to do it? I know how you must be fillin' with what you told me about seeing Marcus, and with him being headed out of town for however long."

"Yeah, Mama," Kayla said. "I'll drive. It ain't no problem. I want you to really think about maybe us takin' you to the emergency room about the side of your head. How is it feelin'? I notice that you keep touchin' it and it had me thinkin'."

"Don't worry about me, Kayla," Rolanda said. "And I told you last night, and this morning, if you remember, that I ain't got no insurance to be goin' to no hospital. And since we might have to be moving soon, I definitely don't need to be going out and gettin' no bills that ain't necessary right now. What little money I got, I'mma need to have."

Kayla looked at her mother, knowing that whatever money she had to her name at this point would be the child support that she received from Latrell and Linell's father every month, which was about $500, her food stamp card, and whatever money she got from whatever nigga she would be lying in bed with in the month. Kayla began to wonder how long it would be before she watched her mama sneaking out the front door in the middle of the night – out of Lyesha's door – to go hang out with some other man. Sure, she was being motherly at the moment. Even the most coldhearted woman would be able to get her act together for all of twenty minutes after going through something as tragic as what they all had gone through last night. However, Kayla also knew that her mother became very complacent, very quickly.

She knew that her mother would probably settle for staying with her friend Lyesha for as long as Lyesha would allow. Sooner or later, however, Lyesha, who was actually working to move up and on with her life, would get tired of a friend and her three kids, one of which is grown, sleeping on her living room couch. How many mornings would she be able to get ready for work and walk passed sleeping bodies in her spare bedroom upstairs as she went to the bathroom? How many mornings would she be able to look passed adult sleeping bodies on her couch in her living room when she was coming downstairs to head out and get downtown to work? How long would she be able to have her utility bills suddenly go up and be okay with it? Kayla, in thinking about all of this, began to get a little bit of a headache.

Soon enough, the four of them were ready. With the key that Rolanda had gotten from Lyesha when she was getting ready for work that morning, Rolanda shuffled her children out of the back door. She set the alarm, then came walking out, catching up to them on the walkway that crossed Lyesha's backyard and went to the gate at the back of the garage. Even though everything was covered in snow, Kayla could tell that Lyesha probably had a really nice backyard during the spring and summer months. There were indentations where patios were buried in snow. Bushes, which looked like rose bushes, lined her brown privacy fence on either side of the yard. There was a picnic table with a letdown umbrella off in the middle of the larger side of the yard. While looking around, all Kayla could think about how these were the things that she would want for herself one day. She just had to get passed this test – this part – and maybe all of that would be possible. Only time would know at this point.

Kayla got in behind the wheel as her mother, brother, and sister climbed into the car also. After allowing the car to warm up for a few minutes, Kayla slowly backed out and into the alley. She headed toward the street, being careful of how hard she pushed the accelerator. The last thing she needed right now was to be getting stuck in the slush that was the alley because of the sun coming out today, in full force for the first time in a while.

When Kayla pulled out onto 36th Street, then headed to the stop sign at Keystone Avenue, she noticed that her mother was looking through her phone. After a couple of glances in her direction, she could see that her mother was scrolling through her text messages. Next thing she knew, her fingers were texting away. Normally, Kayla would not give one shit who her mother was texting. However, she had a strange feeling that her mother was about to do something that would make her life even harder than it already was. Of course, she could not be sure of this. She would just have to wait and see.

By the time Kayla was headed down 38th Street to head back to the west side of the city, Latrell and Linell had basically fallen into a back and forth conversation with one another. Kayla missed being the young, sometimes. To have so little understanding of the world around you was so nice – a feeling that she really missed right now.

"Kayla," Rolanda said, clearly wanting to get her undivided attention. "I wanted to run something passed you."

Fuck, Kayla thought. She wanted to roll her eyes so badly at that moment. What is she about to say to me right now? What the fuck she got to run by me?

"Yeah?" Kayla said, glancing over at her mother then back at the street ahead of her.

"I wanted to know what you thought of me letting y'all daddy keep Latrell and Linell for a while," Rolanda said. "What you think? I mean, as far as I know, he ain't got no crazy shit goin'. Sure, I don't like that bitch he call a girlfriend. But, I gotta get these kids somewhere. When Lyesha get home from work today, I'mma talk to her and see what she say about how long we can stay there until I figure out what we gon' do, or come up with some money or whatever. I just wanted to know what you thought of something like that."

Kayla took a moment to think about it. Since her mother and father had broken up, her mother had truly been on a downward spiral. The divorce hit her so hard, as Kayla only learned why as she got older and grew from a teenage girl, watching her parents get a divorce, to a young woman that had to learn how to maneuver this thing called life. Kayla had learned that her mother's self-worth was tied in to whatever man she was with. And seeing her marriage fall apart, which was partly her fault no matter what she would tell people when she was out and about, was definitely a learning experience for Kayla.

"Have you talked to Daddy, yet?" Kayla asked. "I mean…You think he is going to be okay with doin' somethin' like that all of the sudden, out of the blue?"

Rolanda shrugged and sighed. "I don't know why he wouldn't be," she said. "I mean, these his damn kids too, ain't they?"

Kayla nodded. "Yeah," she said, in agreeing.

"Exactly," Rolanda said. "If I gotta take care of them every day of the week, for years and years, why can't his ass do it for like two or three months or whatever time I need to come up with some money?"

Kayla held back another instinct to roll her eyes after hearing the words that had just come out of her mother's mouth only inches away from her.

"Well," Kayla said. "Have you talked to Daddy and see what he say? I mean, yeah, it sound like a good idea. It would definitely be better than all of us stayin' with Lyesha like this."

"Right," Rolanda said, glad that somebody was agreeing with her. "That is exactly what I was thinkin'. And no, I ain't talked to him yet. I sent him a text, but he ain't responded yet. He prolly at work or whatever, so I'mma not text him until later on this evening or something. Maybe I'll call him or some shit."

"So," Kayla said. "If Daddy agree to let Latrell and Linell come stay with him and stuff for a couple months, what does that mean for me and you?"

"Girl," Rolanda said, looking over at her daughter. "You grown. I know you ain't been havin' the best luck with finding a job, but you ain't really been lookin' like you should be lookin', either. I know you don't think that I listen and shit, but I do. I do, Kayla. And I'm tellin' you that you need to get a little more aggressive with lookin' for a job. You can't just keep laying around my house or with your boyfriend, who is on his way out of town or wherever right now, forever."

So bad, at that very moment, Kayla wanted to pull her car over. Right there, on 38th Street, which was a wide, busy street without parking on either side, Kayla wanted to pull into the right lane and slam on her damn breaks. She wanted to tell her mother how she really felt, how she was not the kind of woman who should be giving anybody in this whole wide world any kind of employment advice. To Kayla, that was like a person who has been married three or four times, for all short periods, trying to give somebody advice on how to keep their marriage going strong. Instead, though, Kayla bit her tongue for a minute. She knew how her mother must have been rattled inside of her head by basically getting pistol whipped. She tried to not take the words that were coming out of her mouth to seriously.

"I know," Kayla said. "But, Mama, you know how hard it is to find a job after the holidays. Ain't nobody really hiring in January and February like that."

"I know, I know," Rolanda said. "But maybe you can get on at McDonalds or somewhere. I feel like when I be ridin' around and shit, I be seein' them McDonald's signs that say NOW HIRING. Have you applied with them? I mean, damn. Anything? Surely some of these restaurants are out here hiring."

Kayla looked out of the window as she drove the car down 38th Street and passed the fairgrounds. She really, truly wanted to let her mother know some things. However, she also knew that she wanted to be the bigger person. She was not going to let her mother get a rise out of her. If Kayla had her way, and her life was not literally going to hell right before her eyes, she would tell her mother that she had no room to talk. Instead, she thought of something else she could say.

"So, what are you sayin', Mama?" Kayla asked. "You wanna go up to a McDonald's and apply together and we both work there until we get a place again or what?"

Rolanda looked over at her daughter and rolled her eyes. She began to shake her head. "Girl, is you serious?" she snapped back. "I ain't bout to be caught dead workin' up in no damn McDonalds or no fast food restaurant. I am too old for that shit, Kayla. I don't even know why you would say something like that."

Kayla was not the least bit surprised by her mother's response. After all, for the last several months – almost a year, really – she had watched her mother come home with money, somehow, but never go to work. Kayla used to joke with Marcus about it, calling it "Rolanda's magic trick." Instead, Kayla simply decided to let the conversation die. She did not even know why her mother asked her what she thought about Latrell and Linell going to stay with her father until they had a place again. The woman had already planned out in her head, probably while she was texting, what she was going to do. She just needed some reassurance, and that is what she got.

Kayla rolled down 38th Street until she turned down Martin Luther King, to head south, toward downtown and toward their neighborhood. The closer she got to where she would be turning to begin zigzagging to their specific street, the more last night would play out in her head. It was like a movie at this point. If it was not like a movie, then it was like a television show that had one horrific episode that would never be forgotten. She could only hope that today would go just fine – that they would be able to run into the house and pack some things quickly. It was not that late into the day, and she liked to think that Hakim's boys, whoever they were, would not be the type of guys to be trying to pull what they pulled last night during daytime hours. Kayla was already thinking ahead, though. She had decided that she would ride around the block before they pulled up out front and headed inside.

Within ten minutes or so, Rolanda had gotten on the phone and had a quick conversation with somebody that Kayla could not make out from what she was saying. When she got off the phone, she went back to being her usual self.

"Alright, Kayla," Rolanda said. "I was thinkin' we ride by first and see if we wanna go in or not. Don't even slow down and stop and look and stuff. Just ride by like you ridin' down the street. And we gotta make sure we lookin' inside of parked cars and shit, looking for niggas who just might be sittin' there. Make sure you say something this time if you see anything like that."

Kayla gave her mother the side-eye before looking back ahead and turning onto Paris. "Okay, Mama," she said. "I will."

They rolled by the front of their house. There were not a lot of cars parked on the block, so it made it relatively easy for them to see if anyone was sitting in their car – if any niggas were sitting and waiting on them to come back. Luck must have been on their side because there was no sign of anyone sitting outside. Once Kayla had rolled around the block, and they had decided against pulling in the back and going in the house, she pulled into a parking spot out front. Myesha popped into her mind some minutes before, but she had noticed that even her car was nowhere to be seen, as she was probably busy with some school activity or another.

"Alright, y'all," Rolanda said. She looked into the rearview mirror, back at Latrell and Linell. "We gon go in here and get them little suitcases y'all used that last time we went outta town, remember?"

Latrell and Linell both said that they remembered what suitcases their mother was talking about, both nodding their head.

"And I want y'all to get five or six outfits and just as many pairs of underwear and some shoes that match multiple outfits, okay?" Rolanda said. "Get that and grab your book bags and whatever else you'll need to go to school and stuff. I wanna make this quick. I ain't try'na be here all day. Get in and get out. No fuckin' around."

As Latrell and Linell agreed, Kayla and Rolanda looked up and down the street one last time. They all started to get out of the car, moving as if nothing was wrong, and heading up toward the front porch. Just as they got halfway across the front yard, Rolanda heard somebody say her name. "Rolanda, girl?" a woman said. "I was just thinkin' bout you."

Quickly, Rolanda and Kayla both looked to their right, in the direction of the voice. Latrell and Linell continued going on, and up to the porch. It was Ms. White, this woman who was nice to Rolanda every day of the week. However, there were times that Rolanda could not stand talking to the woman. She was one of those neighbors who were just so damn nice that it was hard to be mean to her. However, she had a habit of talking somebody's ear off and holding them up with all of her pleasantries. Now, of course, was definitely not the time for a Ms. White talk.

Rolanda forced a smile, showing the fakest side of her personality. "Hi Ms. White," she said, waving. "How you been?"

Ms. White, who was probably just a little past sixty years old and known for being black and mixed with some sort of Native American, walked down her walkway and down the sidewalk. She now stood only feet from Kayla and Rolanda.

"I'm okay, Miss White," Rolanda said.

Kayla spoke, waving. "Hi Miss White," she said. "How you doin'?"

"I'm alright, I'm alright," Ms. White said. "Like I was sayin', I was worried about y'all if you really wanna know why I came out."

"Oh," Rolanda said, trying to sound surprised. "Really?"

"Yeah," Ms. White said, the medium height, thin woman nodding her head. "I saw that it was y'all pullin' up and I decided to get on some clothes and run out here. Is everything okay? I heard what sounded like a gunshot last night, or so I thought, and I wasn't too sure where it was coming from. I thought it was you all."

Rolanda and Kayla, at the very same time, could instantly feel both of their hearts thump very hard in their chest. They had gotten so caught up in the whirlwind that was last night that they had not thought much about the idea of somebody hearing the gunshot last night. Rolanda wanted to curse so badly that the words almost slipped right on out of her mouth.

"Yeah," Rolanda said, smiling. "That was an accident, actually. We had a little scare from a cousin of ours, and I am not happy about it."

Kayla stood there, really wondering where her mother was taking Ms. White with this story. Ms. White showed a very concerned face, letting them know that she wanted to know more.

"Yeah, Miss White," Rolanda said. "I don't know if you saw, but we had a couple of cousins come over earlier. Girl, I am so mad about that. One of them had a gun and it went off."

"Oh no," Ms. White said, holding her hand up over her mouth. She looked at Kayla and Rolanda, then passed them and up at Latrell and Linell, who were waiting by the door. "I hope nobody got hurt."

Kayla could see Ms. White's eyes leaning up at this point and toward her mother. She was looking at the wound on the side of her mother Rolanda's head.

"Yeah," Rolanda said. "We were just a little spooked is all."

"Oh...," Ms. White said. "Okay. Girl, what happened to your head?"

"Tripped on the steps," Rolanda said, lying.

Kayla noticed how good of a storyteller her mother was at this very moment. After all, the woman did indeed have years, at this point, of experience. She was clearly using every bit of it right now. It was almost impressive how good of a liar her mother was.

"Yeah," Rolanda said. "I tripped comin' down the steps, thinkin' I was young like I used to be. I feel right on down and hit by head. It hurt, but I'm just cut. It ain't as bad as it looked."

"Alright, baby," Ms. White said. "I just figured I would come on out here and ask."

"We comin' y'all!" Rolanda said to Latrell and Linell, hearing that one of them had called her name. She turned back to her neighbor. "Miss White," she said. "I'd hate to cut this short, but we gotta get going. We've got some other things we need to do today, and this wind out here ain't no joke."

"Of course, of course," Ms. White said, beginning to walk away and back toward her walkway. "Girl, call me sometime. Don't forget to let me know if you need anything."

"I will," Rolanda said, walking away and toward the front door.

Kayla waved by to Ms. White as she went back over to her front yard and headed up to her front porch. She truly wondered if Ms. White had bought the story that her mother had just given her – the lies that her mother had wrapped up like nice, big late Christmas presents.

Soon enough, Rolanda and Kayla were leading the way as the four of them stepped into the living room. Even though the room was dimly lit, it was obvious as soon as they stepped all the way inside. The two niggas who had held them at gunpoint last night had come back. The apartment looked trashed. The television was on the floor, rather than stolen. The fish tank was knocked over and sitting on its side on the floor with the different color fish spread out across the floor. Instantly, they all could not help but to feel nervous – to feel violated. Even their family pictures, which were perfectly framed and each had their own spot on the wall, were now spread about the floor. It was obvious that they had dug the heel of their shoes into the pictures, judging by the way that the glass was smashed.

As soon as Rolanda pushed the door closed, feeling lucky that no cars had rolled by while they were outside talking to Ms. White, she began to move forward in the house.

"Let me make sure ain't nobody in here," she said. "Y'all wait right here."

Kayla waited with Latrell and Linell, who both looked up at her with the eyes of confused young children. She felt so sorry for them right then that she shook her head, almost wanting to cry even if they were not crying. Within a few minutes, their mother had returned, appearing to be much more relaxed after checking out the entire house.

"Alright, y'all," Rolanda said. "Let's make this quick."

***

It only took them all about ten minutes to get the basic necessities together. At this time, they were huddled in the living room with Rolanda trying to make sure that Latrell and Linell were good to go. Kayla, too, had gone upstairs and packed some things into a duffle bag. All the while she moved around her bedroom, then around the house, she could not help but to think about Marcus. He truly was the love of her life. And she really hoped that whatever he was calling himself going to do would not make his problems even worse. She reminded herself to text him back when they all got back into the car. She found herself feeling much more relaxed in the living room now, compared to last night.

"We got everything?" Rolanda asked, out loud, after picking up a few family photos that had been smashed on the dining room floor. She shook the broken glass off of them before sliding them into her pocket.

Everyone said they had everything that they had come from. Rolanda motioned for them to head toward the door. "Come on, y'all," she said. "Let's go on and get on outta here."

As soon as Kayla opened the front door, she found herself having to catch her breath. None of them had thought to look outside before opening the front door, especially since the living room window was angled in such a way to where they could look pretty far down the street.

"What? What?" Rolanda asked, sounding very concerned. She moved Latrell and Linell out of the way and stepped up to the door. There, she saw it as well: a black car rolling by. At this point, the car had basically passed by their yard and was heading down the street. However, out reflex, they all backed back into the house.

"Was that the same car?" Rolanda asked Kayla. She then looked down to Latrell and Linell, remembering that they had seen the car ride by yesterday when they were playing out in the snow. "Tell me, y'all. Was that the same car?"

Latrell shook his head then Linell did the same. They both said, almost at the very same time, that they did not see whatever car Kayla and their mother had just seen when Kayla opened the front door.

"Fuck, fuck, fuck," Rolanda said. She then looked to her grown daughter. "Girl, what was you thinkin'?" she asked.

"What, Mama?" Kayla asked, not knowing where her mother was going with that kind of question.

"What you mean what I mean, Kayla?" Rolanda asked. "Why you ain't at least look out the window before you pulled that damn front door open? Why you ain't look first, huh? Was that the same car as them two niggas from last night or no, girl?"

Kayla, hating that her mother blamed her for that mishap, shook her head. "I don't know," she answered. "When I pulled up last night, it was so dark outside and I rushed in so quick because of what y'all had said when you called me that I ain't really look at the car like that, Mama. I don't know if that was the car or not."

"Girl, you a trip," Rolanda said, putting her hands on her hips and shaking her head.

Just then, Kayla watched as her mother stepped over to the living room window behind where the television once sat. Rolanda checked outside, looking both ways.

"I don't see whoever it was coming back around the block or nothin'," Rolanda said. "Let's hurry up and get the fuck outta here before some shit pop off. That shit last night got us all paranoid. It was probably just somebody ridin' down the street or something."

Kayla shrugged it off as well to being paranoid. On that note, Kayla quickly pulled the front door open. The four of them rushed out into the cold once again. Rolanda, on full alert, pull the front door to her house closed and locked it. Within less than a minute's time, they all had rushed down the walkway and were quickly getting into the car after putting their packed bags into the trunk.

Inside, Rolanda looked over at her daughter. "Come on, girl," she said to Kayla, the look on her face letting her know that she was really feeling some kind of way about her opening the door before looking. "Let's get the fuck on up outta here. I can't believe you."

Really having to bite her tongue and prevent herself from saying what she really wanted to say, Kayla put the car into drive and carefully pulled out of the parking spot. For whatever reason, the eye on the left side of her face – on the side of her face that faced away from her mother – let a tear out. Kayla could feel it, as the side of her face was somewhat cold from having just been out in the cold, Indiana wind, as it rolled down the side of her face. Never in her life had she felt so guilty as she did right then. And the crazy thing about it was that she did not even do anything wrong to cause her family to wind up in this kind of situation.

Chapter 6

When Marcus and his mother were rolling into what was known as the Fort Wayne Metropolitan, it was immediately clear to Marcus that he would not be living the big city life that he had been used to for his entire life. While Fort Wayne, Indiana is somewhat big, especially compared to the many of the small towns that scatter the state, it is certainly nowhere close to the size of Indianapolis. Upon getting off the Interstate 90, however, Marcus did get a little feeling of relief. There were at least black people.

"At least they got some niggas up here," Marcus said out loud, and not necessarily talking directly to his mother.

Lorna shook her head. "I ain't bringing you up here to hang out with no niggas, Marcus," she said. "Remember what I told you. I don't want this getting any worse than it already is. Don't worry about who is or is not here, cause everywhere has those kind of people. I want you to keep your ass out of these streets up here and to get onto the right path. Ain't got time for no more bullshit. I swear I don't."

"I know, Mama," Marcus said. "I know."

Just then, Marcus looked back down at his cell phone. He was wondering why for the last hour and a half or so of their drive up from Indianapolis, Kayla had not yet responded to his text message. He still was unsure of what he was going to say to his boys Brandon and Juan. As much as he could tell that his mother severely mistrusted both of them, Marcus trusted in himself. Brandon and Juan had been his boys – practically like brothers to him – for a while now. The further and further he got away from Indianapolis, the more guilt that came over him because he knew that he was purposely ignoring their texts from earlier in the day because of what his mother had said. He contemplated changing all of that, but he wanted to get wherever he was going right now first. Then, and only then, he would start plotting, no matter how fucked up his arm was from being shot in the shoulder.

Lorna exited the highway and they began to make their way through Fort Wayne. Marcus had to admit to himself that he was indeed a little surprised. As they drove closer into the city, seeing some ghetto areas as well as some nicer areas, then the small cluster of mid-rises and high-rises that made up Downtown Fort Wayne, the city was actually a little bigger than he expected.

Marcus looked ahead, taking in the scenery as he smoked. "Do you even know where this nigga lives, Mama?" Marcus asked. "Do you know where we goin' or what?"

"Sort of," Lorna answered, looking around. She then glanced at the time above her car stereo. She thanked God that they were able to drive from Indianapolis to Fort Wayne without running into any kind of traffic that would slow them down. She was so sure that God would throw them another challenge, but once again, he had come through for her and her son. "I used to come up to Fort Wayne when I was younger. You know, some of your cousins and stuff used to live up here before parts of the family started to move down south. We used to come up here to see them, especially when I was a child. We came up here sometimes when I got grown, when you were a baby really. In fact, before your daddy up and disappeared, I remember than him and me had come up here. But the city definitely looks different now than it looked back then. I don't remember it looking this big."

Marcus chuckled as he looked around at the inner-city neighborhoods that they passed through. "Big," he said, sarcastically. "I mean, it ain't no little town. But I wouldn't call it big like that."

"Well, Marcus," Lorna said. "It was a lot smaller than this when I was coming up here, back in the day. Some of these buildings downtown were here, like the older ones, but it looks like it has filled in a bit cause I definitely can't say that I remember a lot of these newer looking buildings."

Marcus nodded.

Just then, the two of them could hear Lorna's phone vibrating. It sounded as if it was coming from the depths of her purse.

"Get my phone out of my purse, Marcus," Lorna told him. "Would you? That is probably your cousin Larry calling to see where we are. I really don't want to make him late for getting back to work or whatever he has to do today, I don't know."

Marcus did just as his mother had asked. He picked his mother's purse up off of the car floor and lifted it into his lap, feeling how heavy it was to just pick up.

"Dang, Mama," he said as he dug around inside, following the vibrations of her phone. "Why is this thing so dang heavy?"

"Just be careful with it, Marcus," Lorna told him. "You know why my purse is heavy. When you put it back onto the floor, make sure that you're gentle when you set it down. We don't need any more bullets going off."

At that moment, Marcus knew exactly what his mother meant. And he was not the least bit surprised that she had pulled her gun out from her "special" hiding place for this trip. Quickly, though, Marcus found his mother's cell phone. As he handed the phone to his mother, he got a glimpse of the lit-up screen. The person calling was indeed his cousin Larry.

"Hello?" Lorna answered.

"Hey cousin, Lorna," Larry said, in his usual pleasant voice. "I just got in the door from work and was wondering how close you and Marcus was."

"I don't know," Lorna answered. "You said that you live up by that mall, right."

"Exactly," Larry said. "I actually live in some apartments that are on the main street, across from the mall. You should see like a retention pond or lake or whatever and you will know that them is my apartments."

Lorna nodded and glanced at Marcus. "Well," she said. "We're not close to the mall right now. We just passed through downtown and now, if I'm not mistaken, I'm heading north on whatever street this is and it should bring me to the mall."

"Are you about to cross over a bridge?" Larry asked.

Lorna looked ahead, looking for sign of some water. Just then, the street bended and she could see that a bridge was coming up. "Yup," she answered. "We sure are. Just about to cross is right now."

"Cool," Larry said. "You remember what apartment? That street that you on will bring you right on up to where the mall is."

"Yeah," Lorna answered. "I remember what street and stuff. Just didn't know exactly where I was. This city has changed a little bit since the last time that I was up here, however many years ago that was."

"Okay, I'll see you when you get here," Larry said. "I'm waiting."

"Okay," Lorna said. "We'll be there in a minute."

When Lorna hung up the phone, Marcus just sat in his seat quietly. He readjusted his arm a little bit because he was starting to feel a little sore in his shoulder. His mother noticed right away.

"Marcus, did you bring that prescription with you?" Lorna asked.

Marcus sighed. "Yeah, Mama," he said. "I did."

"Okay," Lorna said. "While you up here, make sure you get to the nearest CVS or Walgreens or whatever and get that filled. Don't be up here smoking no weed because you think that it'll help with your pain or whatever bullshit niggas be talking nowadays."

Marcus looked over at his mother and how serious her face looked. He knew that he needed to say something that was comical to somewhat break the ice. "Dang, Mama," he said and smiled.

Lorna glanced over at her son. "Dang, what, Marcus?" she asked.

"You knew my plan so well, didn't you," Marcus said, sounding rhetorical.

Lorna gave her son the side eyed look. "Alright, now, Marcus," she said. "Wind up in jail or some shit up here and I swear to God that I'mma just let your ass sit there. I'mma just let you sit there. Try me if you want to."

"I know, Mama," Marcus said, starting to feel like a broken record. "I know."

Lorna continued steering the car through the north side of Fort Wayne until she came to the road with the mall. At this point, she could spot the equivalent of maybe five or six city blocks down the road, what looked like a lake with some apartments next to it.

"There," she said, pointing in the direction of the lake, which was on the other side of the mall parking lot. "Your cousin Larry lives over there. Those are his apartments."

Now that Marcus was finally within eyesight of his destination, he could get a real feel for where he would be living. He looked around, in silence, not wanting to say anything because anything that he said would be turned around and used against him. He liked that he would be able to walk not too far to get to a mall. It would be different compared to Indianapolis, where he had a car to drive, but it was starting to look like the kind of place that he could work with. At least he would not have to walk far to get to a store and whatnot.

Within a couple of minutes, they were turning off of the main road and heading down a bending road that went alongside the edges of the retention pond. Lorna looked at the address numbers on the street signs, so that she would know what street to turn onto to get to Larry's part of the complex. Once she found the right sign, she turned and soon enough they were pulling into a parking spot that was directly outside of the door that led in to where Larry lived. Lorna felt relieved, knowing that her child was no at least a good two and a half hours away from whoever was trying to blow his damn head off. This was the first feeling of relief that she had felt in the last day or so, since she got the call at work from Kayla that Marcus had been shot in the drive by.

Marcus climbed out of the car as Lorna called inside to Larry and told him that they were outside. He opened the backseat doors and pulled out his bag of clothes and whatnot, which proved to be harder than he had originally thought, considering that he was now using just one arm instead of two. Within seconds, Marcus saw that his cousin Larry was walking out of the door to his apartment building and headed down the walkway.

Larry was what many would describe as a teddy bear kind of guy. He was tall and kind of husky looking with a beard that was almost the size of Rick Ross'. Lorna smiled as she hugged him, saying thank you.

"Thank you for doing this," Lorna said to Larry. "I really, really do appreciate it."

"Oh, no problem," Larry said, as the broke their hug off. "No problem."

Marcus and Larry then looked to one another. They shook hands like two cousins would, then hugged one another.

"Hey, wassup man?" Marcus said, trying to smile and be happy about being here in the first place. "What's been up with you?"

"Just working," Larry said. He then grabbed the bag from Marcus, who had basically been dragging it from the backseat of his mother's car and up onto the sidewalk. Out of instinct, Larry wanted to ask Marcus how he was doing, but he knew that doing such a thing would only be sprinkling salt on his fresh wound. When Lorna had called Larry and told him what all happened, as well as what she thought of it all, Larry picked right up on how serious the situation was. "Let's get on inside," Larry said. "It's cold out here, and I think that it's supposed to start snowing again later on, but I don't know."

On that note, Larry let Marcus and his mother into his apartment building and upstairs to his apartment. Before going into the door, however, Marcus made sure to get a good look around at the kind of people that were going in and out of the doors of other apartment buildings. From the looks of it, his cousin was doing pretty well for himself. Marcus saw a lot of older white people going into the buildings.

Once they got into Larry's apartment, Larry pushed the door closed. "This is it," he said, referring to his apartment.

Marcus looked around, noticing how his cousin had an apartment that was just about as nice as his. However, he also thought about how his cousin had gotten his by working a job, rather than dealing drugs like he did.

"Oh, okay," Lorna said, looking around. "Ain't nothing wrong with it, ain't nothing wrong with this."

Larry walked over to his kitchenette and came back with a key. He handed the key to his cousin Marcus and began to explain.

"As you saw," Larry said. "There is no key to get into the building. Here is the key to the door and stuff. The kitchen is over there, as you see, and I got my extra room ready for you. I was using it as like a home office, but I moved some stuff around to make room for you."

Marcus nodded as he grabbed the key. "Yeah," Marcus said. "Thanks man."

Marcus walked passed his mother and Larry and made his way to the bedroom hallway and back to the two bedroom doors. Immediately, he could see which room was his. On one side of the hallway was a larger bedroom that had what looked like a pretty good sized bed and some nice, wood furniture to match. On the other side, however, was smaller room. Marcus pushed the door open, pulling his bag behind him then dropping it just inside the door. He flipped on the light and saw how his cousin Larry had indeed somewhat rearranged the room, with his desk on one side next to some boxes and papers that looked like files.

After Marcus looked around his room for a while, and realized how much different staying with his cousin would be compared to living on his own like he was used to doing, he went back out to the living room. He walked up to his mother and Larry.

"Thank you, man," Marcus said, knowing that his mother was expecting him to say something. "Thank you for the room."

Lorna looked back to Larry. "I hope we didn't hold you up from getting back to work or whatever," she said.

"Naw," Larry said, shaking his head. He checked the time on his phone. "I betta get back to work, though. My supervisor is the kind of guy that will come calling and stuff, trying to see where I am."

"I understand," Lorna said. She looked at Larry and what he had done for himself – done without having to sell an ounce of any drugs out in the streets. "You go on and get back to work. Once again, thank you. I'm going to get back onto the road soon, before it gets too late. Plus, I don't want to be driving back and into Indianapolis when it's dark, especially if it might snow."

On that note, Larry hugged his cousin Lorna once more and told Marcus that he would be back around 6 o'clock. He left out of the apartment and headed back down stairs to get back to work. Once again, Marcus was in the room alone with his mother. The two of them looked around.

"Well," Lorna said, as she sat down on a couch. "This don't look too bad, do it?"

Marcus shook his head. "Naw," he answered. "It don't."

"Let me just rest for a second before I head back," Lorna said. "So, Marcus, what's on your mind? Tell me what you're thinking about?"

Marcus took a moment to answer. Out of instinct, he tried to shrug his shoulders. He soon winced, upon feeling the stiffness, and began to readjust his arm.

"Nothin'," Marcus answered. "Just thinkin' about stayin' up here now, in this apartment. And Kayla. Mama?"

"What?" Lorna asked, wanting to know.

"When do you think you'll be coming back up here?" Marcus asked.

Lorna looked away. "I don't know," she answered. "I know when I get back, I will call and talk to your uncle for a minute. Which reminds me, I need to call him and remind him that we made it. I'll call him when I get out to the car. Maybe I can come back up here next week or something."

Marcus walked around the dining room area, then looked in and around the kitchenette and bathroom. "Yeah," he said. "I guess this place will be coo…for a little while."

After about ten minutes of sitting on Larry's couch, allowing her body to relax a little bit, Lorna pressed the palms of her hands into her thighs and stood up.

"Well," Lorna said. "I betta get back on the road before the weather gets bad again or something."

"Okay, Mama," Marcus said, still absorbing what would be his new home for a while. "Thank you for bringing me up here."

Lorna hugged her son, in a way that she would when he was a little boy and going away for the weekend with family or something. "Marcus, please remember what I told you," she said to him. "Please remember what I told you. Watch who you hang out with. Don't be getting involved in any other crap while you're up here with your cousin. And, most importantly, I don't care what you think of your little buddies. Do not tell them where you are. Come up with something else to say, but don't be telling them so that the wrong people find out where you are and can come find you."

"Okay, Mama," Marcus said. "Okay."

When his mother broke away from her hug, she said bye to Marcus and walked out of the door. Within seconds, Marcus had heard her footsteps going down the steps and her car starting then pulling out of the driveway. Marcus finally chilled out for a little while, liking that he was alone after the drive up from Indianapolis.

"This is some fucked up shit," he said to himself as he began to feel angry. He did not like that Hakim was really doing the most with this. At the same time, he knew that he only made things worse by smashing Hakim's chick. That was all in the past now, just like his mother had said.

Marcus chilled out for a second. Next thing he knew, as he was starting to lean back and doze off right there on his cousin Larry's couch, his phone was vibrating. He quickly pulled it out of his pocket, assuming that it was Kayla. The person calling was not Kayla, however. Rather, it was his Uncle Roy. Marcus smiled and answered, happy to finally talk to the one nigga that had basically been by his side his entire life.

"Wassup, Uncle?" Marcus said.

"Wassup," Roy responded, talking quietly. "Is your mother around you?"

CPSIA information can be obtained
at www.ICGtesting.com
Printed in the USA
LVOW07s1717210917
549566LV00010B/915/P